JEKKA WILDE

KING OF CLUBS

THE WICKED BOYS OF WONDERLAND

BOOK TWO

ISBN: 978-1-964291-05-5

CONTENTS

ONE

ALICE

The King of Clubs was laughing at me.

Not in an obnoxious, drunk frat boy at the comedy club kind of way, but in a twisted, sinister, wicked kind of way.

He'd tricked me.

The douchelord had *tricked* me! He'd kidnapped me and stolen the Vorpal Sword from me, and now he'd just tricked me into making a deal to stay with him until he said otherwise.

For all I knew, that might be forever.

Fuck my life.

Right in the ass.

With a traffic cone.

"That's not fair!" I screamed at him. "You asshole! I never had a chance of leaving, did I? That's not fair at all!"

"I don't play fair, Alice," said the King of Clubs as he returned to the black velvet sofa and resumed his card game with Callister. "I play to *win*."

It took me a hot second to pick my jaw back up from where it had fallen on the floor. I'd been screwed over so many times in my life that I'd lost count. People had taken advantage of my family's fame and money and connections, but this was some next level shit.

I had a closet full of Birkin bags, Miu Miu, and Prada. I drove a fucking Bentley. When I wanted a table at the hottest restaurant, I didn't need reservations. I always got the best seat. Same with movie premiers and music festivals. I only sat in the VIP section. I'd been to the Met Gala *twice*. I never had to wait in line for anything . . . not even Taylor Swift tickets.

Wherever I went, people fell over themselves to kiss my ass, impress me, or make my life easier. According to my now missing Cheshire Cat demon and Mad Hatter, I was also the Ace of Spades to Wonderland.

I was Alice Fucking Darling, and I wasn't about to put up with the King of Clubs' bullshit for another second.

Wonderland wasn't even *real*!

I was only here because I'd had too much to drink and followed a guy dressed like the White Rabbit through the streets of LA so I could return his stupid pocket watch. I must've slipped in the rain and hit my head.

Or maybe I'd simply blacked out and my personal assistant Dinah had stuffed me in an Uber and dragged me back home. I knew the second I got out of this black room full of big fancy mirrors, I'd wake up in my own bedroom and vow to never get so wasted again.

I marched across the polished black and gold tiles of the king's private apartment and wrapped my hands around the ornate golden doorknob.

It didn't budge.

With all my might, I heaved and twisted and yanked. Then I tried pushing as hard as I could.

Nothing.

My hands were starting to hurt.

"Should we tell her it's locked?" Callister asked, glancing over his hand of cards until his gaze met the king's.

The King of Clubs revealed a faint smile as I spun around to glare at him. He'd be gorgeous if he wasn't such an insufferable prick.

"I think she's figured it out."

"Let me go!" I demanded. "I'm not your prisoner!"

"On the contrary," the king murmured as he casually added more gold poker chips to the existing stack on the table between him and Callister. He tossed down a card, then looked up at me. "That's *exactly* what you are."

"You can't keep me here forever!"

"I can keep you as long as I want. You and I made a deal. I didn't get to where I am by going back on my word."

Full of righteous indignation, my eyes flashed with anger.

"Your *word*? Your word doesn't mean *shit*! You *lied* to me!"

He leaned back on the velvet sofa, bringing his cards close to his chest before his dark eyes flicked up to me.

"Sit," he commanded, gesturing to the empty space next to him.

"Not until you tell me where I am."

He let out a soft chuckle and shook his head.

"You don't call the shots in my club, Alice. *I* do. Now sit."

"Go to Hell!"

I watched as the King of Clubs calmly set down his hand of cards and rose smoothly to his feet. Exuding all the power and danger of a panther, he stalked over to where I stood. The Vorpal Sword shone in the candlelight from where it hung on his hip.

He was just as tall as Hatter, and I could tell that underneath the perfectly tailored black three-piece suit was an equally flaw-less body. If I punched him, there was a good chance my hand would feel nothing but rock-hard muscle.

I crossed my arms and jutted out my chin, glaring up at him as if my Malibu-born-and-raised brand of entitled reality TV star bitchiness alone would stop him from whatever he was about to do.

It usually worked with most people.

The King of Clubs wasn't most people.

He wasn't even *human*.

He had fangs. Not huge ones, but the white canines bared to me weren't normal. Did Wonderland have vampires?

I was about to find out.

"What did you just say to me?" he asked in a low growl. But instead of looking angry, I could clearly see something inside of him light up with excitement at my choice of words.

Whatever this display of power was, I knew it was all for show. Guys like him—guys who wore pinky rings like he did—always had something to prove. It was obvious that this was all being done to put me—a woman—in my place.

Who cared if he was butthurt? There was no way he'd actually hurt me in front of Callister. Snickering to myself, I rolled my eyes at the king, then repeated myself so that he wouldn't misunderstand a single word.

"I said: Go. To. Hell."

His cold, calculating eyes suddenly lit up with bright flames of gold.

"Oh, darling . . . I was born there," he hissed through a twisted grin, revealing his pointed teeth. "I was going to go easy on you, but I might as well skip the formalities and give you a taste of what's to come."

I didn't have time to think of a bitchy comeback.

I didn't have time to do anything.

I watched in horror as he brought his hands out in front of his body and pulled off what I could only describe as an invisible cloak. A scream lodged in my throat as the sharp scent of ozone and brimstone assaulted my senses. My heart pounded wildly, fear coursing through my veins.

Two pairs of twisted black horns were now jutting out of his head—the set above his forehead was smaller and pointed up and back, while the set coming from above his pointed ears was massive and curled like they belonged to a demonic ram.

The suit jacket and gold vest disappeared from his body, revealing a collection of esoteric symbols tattooed on his muscular chest and arms. Then a massive pair of leathery black wings unfurled behind him. They beat in unison, sending a few gusts of air through the room.

I was already running towards the bed. I dove underneath to hide from the hellish monster.

It was no use.

A powerful hand shot under the bed, grabbing my ankle in an iron grip. I shrieked as my silk nightgown rode up my thighs when he dragged me out from under the bed and across the floor. My body slid against the polished marble tiles like a raindrop dripping down a window.

He flipped me onto my back and crawled on top of me, his massive weight pressing me into the unforgiving marble and pinning me in place.

He loomed over me, his huge wings furled around him like a billowing cloak . . . his horns curling around him head like a satanic crown.

And all the while, he was grinning in satisfaction like he actually *enjoyed* seeing how terrified I was of him.

Like he fed on my screams and my fear to survive.

The sick fuck.

I beat my fists against his chest, but it didn't seem to affect him at all.

If anything, he reveled in my struggle.

"I could take you right now . . . hard . . . and without mercy," he murmured while gloating from above. His hair hung in his dark eyes like the gorgeous devil or demon I suspected he might be. His fingernails raked against my skin like gentle claws, coaxing a flood of heat into my core. "But that would be too easy.

I know it's only a matter of time before you beg me to fuck you. All the bad bunnies do. You're no exception."

My whole body trembled. Whether it was from terror or arousal, I couldn't say.

His black wings pumped a few times before folding neatly behind his muscled shoulders. He reached out a strong bare arm and I fully expected him to remember who I was—Alice Fucking Darling.

I waited for him to be a gentleman and help me to my feet. Nope.

That hand went straight for the nape of my neck and grabbed a fistful of my tangled blonde hair. Then my face was partially covered by a form-fitting mask.

The moment I thought about taking if off, something strong, yet soft wrapped around my wrists and bound them together behind my back. The movement thrust my shoulders back and my tits up.

The sound of fabric being torn filled my ears until the black silk nightgown I'd been wearing fell away, leaving me completely naked and exposed to both men. Every scratch and bite and bruise and hickey from my three-way fuckfest with Chess and Hatter was now painfully visible to Callister and his monster friend.

The same material that was wrapped around my face and my wrists now encircled my neck. I was wearing a collar . . . a fucking *collar* with a black leather leash. I caught a glimpse of myself in one of the dozen huge mirrors and realized I was wearing a leather bunny mask.

I looked like a complete and utter fuck toy.

What the hell had I just gotten myself into?

Cool air washed over my bare skin as the King of Clubs dragged me by the leash over to the couch. I fought against him . . . but I may as well have been tied to a tow truck.

When the King of Clubs sat down on his couch, I was

6

convinced he was going to drag me over and make me suck his
dick. It wasn't until he pulled my body over his knees that I
understood what I was in for.

"What are you doing?" I demanded as I struggled.

"Teaching you a lesson," he said, holding me down effortlessly. His charismatic smile didn't reach his smoldering dark
eyes. "Bad bunnies need to be punished."

"You're just the demon to do it," Callister agreed with a
wicked laugh.

Fuck . . . this guy really *was* a demon!

A hard hand came down on my rear with a loud smack. I
heard the sound fill the room before I felt the sting spread across
my ass.

When I finally felt the sheer, sharp slap of his hand, I yelped
for mercy.

Another smack reverberated off over the gold framed mirrors
in that dimly-lit room. Cherry tobacco crackled from Callister's
cigarette before it wafted over to my nose. He was watching with
a smirk, clearly enjoying his front seat to the show.

I howled at the pain, at the humiliation, squirming defiantly
against the demon king's inhumanly strong grip as his hand came
down again . . .

And again . . .

And *again.*

My ass burned so hot that I wondered if I was bleeding, but I
refused to cry. I was more angry than hurt. More humiliated than
actually in pain.

My heart leaped when I caught sight of the Vorpal Sword
glinting from the scabbard still wrapped around his hip. It was
the only thing that could save Wonderland, and I'd worked so
hard to find it.

If I was trapped in this bizarre dream, I may as well commit
to it.

The sword was so close . . . and yet, so far beyond my grasp.

I had to get it back.

I had to find Chess and Hatter.

We had to get to the White Queen's castle so I could train with the White Knight and learn how to kill the Jabberwocky. Once it was dead, the Red Queen's dark powers would fade away. Wonderland would return to normal, and then I'd wake up and be back home.

That was the plan.

I couldn't do any of that if I was being held prisoner by the powerful, arrogant King of Clubs.

His hand slapped my ass once more and bounced off, waiting for me to squirm. But the less I resisted his punishment, the more that skillful hand caressed my curves instead of spanking them.

Another slap landed on my other cheek, the sting sinking into my flesh, making my whole body tingle. His hand traced along my shoulder blades...his fingertips soft against my skin. I whimpered, my hips arching of their own accord. I found myself mortified to feel wetness pooling between my legs.

The king took a deep breath and growled with approval, kneading the globes of my ass. "You like this, don't you, Alice? Being spanked and humiliated in front of an audience." His nails pricked my skin, and I shuddered. "Admit it. Tell us how much you love being punished."

I buried my face in the cushions, heat engulfing my entire body. He was right, though I could hardly bear to say it. There was something deeply arousing about being at the mercy of this powerful being, helpless and exposed with Callister's gaze wandering all over my naked body.

The king brought his hand down again, harder this time. I moaned, the pain translating to more tingles of pleasure as it radiated through me.

"Well?" He jerked the leash. "Tell us, or I won't stop."

I turned my head to the side, glancing at Callister. Our eyes met, and I saw my own lust reflected in his gaze.

The king's hand was firm, yet soft to the touch, and I shuddered in relief with every second his palm rested against my skin. It felt so good that I didn't even care that Callister had a perfect view of my bare ass.

A single finger traced the contours of my upper thighs, and I arched my back without thinking. I wanted that finger inside of me. He was a monster, an abomination, and yet part of me wanted to call his bluff.

Go ahead, you fucking monster . . . I thought. *Take me right now. Hard. Without mercy.*

"Tell us, Alice," the king repeated. "Tell us how much you enjoy this."

I lifted my head and tilted my chin upward.

"It's alright."

A look of warning met my gaze, but the flecks of gold were still there, peeking out at me from behind his loose dark hair.

The wings and the horns were still there, too.

So was his nose. I watched his nostrils waver as he scented the air between his nose and my wet pussy.

He shot me a look that said all I needed to know.

He could smell me.

"Just alright?"

In that moment, I knew I hadn't even begun to test the limits of this demon's patience.

"Fine—I like it," I hissed through my teeth. I glanced away from him, my face flaming with humiliation.

"Now, then . . . I asked you to sit down. Do I need to ask you a third time?"

Pursing my lips, I shook my head, and the king loosened up his grip on my leash. I crawled off his lap and reluctantly took my seat beside him, perching gingerly on the edge of the sofa.

Callister looked on, a strange mix of satisfaction and envy in his cruel eyes.

"It burns, doesn't it?" he taunted in between pink puffs on his

9

cherry cigarette. "You should've listened to Ransom the first time he asked you to sit down. I'm glad you didn't."

I immediately glanced at the King of Clubs, blinking with renewed indignation.

Ransom?

The name of the demon holding me hostage was fucking *Ransom*? Oh, the irony. But what a panty-melting name. It matched those panty-melting eyes.

I bit down on my lip before I said something out loud and got more than a spanking.

It wasn't that I was afraid of what Ransom would do to me.

I just didn't want to give Callister the satisfaction of watching it being done.

"Don't bite your lip," Ransom scolded with a slow, predatory smile. It curled just enough to reveal his sharp canine teeth. "That's *my* job now."

I dropped my gaze and found myself staring at an impressive bulge in his black pants that hadn't been there before.

Fuck me . . .

The King of Clubs was serving up mafia devil-daddy realness and I was here for it. He was simultaneously terrifying, yet gorgeous.

He acted like he kept bad bunny girls on leashes all the time, and yet somehow, that spanking session had turned him on.

I'd turned him on.

I knew I was hot, but he was a *demon king*!

Despite my inner feminist screaming that I was no man's property—or demon's for that matter—I felt a strange sense of pride for making him hard. More heat rushed between my thighs. I detested the man, but that didn't stop me from wanting him to want me.

I bet he fucked like a stallion.

Damn.

Now I was even wetter.

I was probably gonna leave a wet spot on his fancy black velvet couch.

In a desperate attempt to ignore the situation, I focused on the room.

The walls were black, and black velvet curtains pooled on the floor, spilling like waterfalls onto the black and gold tiles. Mirrors framed in gold covered the walls and even the ceiling, reflecting various angles of the luxurious bed.

I guess if Ransom liked to put leashes and collars on his bad bunnies, it wasn't a stretch for him to have mirrors all over the walls and the ceiling.

The furniture was carved from ebony, and the candlelight filling the space reflected off the multiple mirrors, flooding the room with a warm, opulent glow.

It was the kind of lighting that always made a naked body look incredible, no matter their skin tone.

"Where am I?" I finally spat out, trying to mask my frustration with bravado. "And why did you kidnap me?"

The flecks of gold in Ransom's mysterious eyes softened and faded. Then he reached out and pulled something I couldn't see over his body. I don't know if it was demon magic or what, but suddenly he was back in his three-piece suit.

All traces of his horns and wings were gone.

But his eyes were exactly the same.

Dark.

Restrained.

Calculating.

With an air of indifference, he tucked his loose strands of hair back into place and picked up his cards from the table. I watched in disbelief as he and Callister resumed their card game as if nothing out of the ordinary had just happened.

"You're in my club . . . The Rabbit Hole." He paused to reveal a wicked smile. "It's where all the bad bunnies of Wonderland come to play."

He watched as Callister picked up a card from the table, frowned at it, then drew another one from the deck. Then another.

"As far as kidnapping you," Ransom went on, "I didn't have much of a choice once the Red Queen learned that you've arrived in Wonderland. There's been a bounty on your head since before you were born. She won't stop searching for you until she has your head on a spike in her rose garden."

"I was safe with Hatter and Chess," I insisted. My wrists were still bound behind my back, and I was still completely naked, tits out, and I was positive that I'd already ruined his couch, but that didn't stop me from trying to act dignified. "You should've seen what they did to the Red Queen's soldiers!"

A low rumble came out of Ransom's chest.

"I know Chess very well. I imagine he tore those soldiers to shreds."

"If you know him so well, then how could you betray him?" I snapped at Ransom before unleashing my anger onto Callister. "And *you*! How could you betray them? Some friend you are! I didn't think you would stoop so low, but I guess I shouldn't be surprised since you're a fucking *worm* shifter!"

Callister's jaw feathered and his mouth twisted into a vicious sneer. He looked like he wanted to punch me.

"I did it to keep them safe," he growled through clenched teeth. "They're the closest thing I have to brothers. Be angry all you want, but I will *not* listen to a spoiled little whore question my loyalty to them!"

"If you're so loyal, then why are you working with this asshole to kidnap me and steal the Vorpal Sword?" I demanded. "That's not part of the plan to save Wonderland!"

Callister's jaw tightened so hard I half expected his teeth to crumble. His gaze flickered over to the king's.

"Are you going to just sit there and let her call you an asshole?"

Ransom shrugged.

"She's not wrong."

Then he turned his attention to me.

"Alice, if you're going to defeat the Red Queen and her Jabberwocky, you must choose your allies with more care. Wonderland is a treacherous place. Not everyone can be trusted to look out for your best interests."

"Hatter and Chess were looking out for me just fine," I insisted.

Ransom traced a warm finger down my cheek, along my collarbone, and between my breasts. Unable to push his hand away, I watched as his touch conjured a trail of goosebumps in its wake. My nipples hardened from the skillful sensation of his touch.

"They may have been looking out for you, but you weren't looking out for them at all," he observed, sincerity lacing his words. "If the Red Queen even *suspects* that either of them knows where you are and they don't tell her, it's off with their heads. I can't have that happening to my friends. Not on my watch."

"Still doubt my loyalty now?" Callister deadpanned in between puffs of pink smoke. There was something undeniably alluring about the darkness within him, a raw vulnerability that tugged at my own desires.

"No," I admitted, "but you could've said something to me instead of having me kidnapped."

Callister's handsome face twisted into a haughty frown.

"I *did* say something to you! I said you're not ready to fight the Red Queen. I don't think you have what it takes to defeat her."

"Quite frankly, neither do I," Ransom murmured, his voice suddenly close to my ear.

He examined his cards and drew from the deck, then elegantly fanned them out and laid them on the table.

Callister let out a contemptuous snort and revealed his hand before tossing down his cards. He shoved all but one of the gold poker chips to Ransom's side of the table. He'd lost the game, but he didn't seem too upset. It was almost like he was expecting to lose all along.

"Alright," I sighed. "I understand why you wouldn't want Chess and Hatter to know where I am, but then why bring me here? Why not take me to the White Queen so I can start learning how to use the Vorpal Sword?"

"Now why the fuck would I bring you to the very first place everyone will look for you?" Callister replied. He tapped his temple and glared at me. "Use your fucking brain, Alice! I know you have one!"

I swallowed hard, feeling like a total moron.

Ransom turned to face me, studying my bunny mask, my hair, my body, yet revealing nothing about his assessment. I found myself praying that he didn't think I was a complete idiot.

"Perhaps Callister realized that you need a king to protect you, not a perpetually drunk fae on the brink of insanity and a Cheshire Cat demon whose power drains away every time he drains his balls in you."

I glanced away, trying to think of a way to deny the accusations.

"Don't bother lying to me, Alice. I can smell him all over you. I can smell both of them. It's perfectly fine if you want to fuck the Cheshire Cat and the Mad Hatter. I'm sure that your cunt was the only thing that made Hatter lucid enough to remember where he hid the Vorpal Sword." He gave the blade at his hip a little pat of safekeeping.

I briefly considered explaining it was actually my *ass* that brought Hatter back to sanity, but it didn't seem like the right time.

"Good job fucking him well enough to find the only weapon that can kill the Jabberwocky," Ransom said as he and Callister rose from their seats. He gave my leash a little tug, and I slowly got up with them as the king showed the grumpy caterpillar to the door.

"Now Chess, on the other hand, would've gotten himself killed if we hadn't taken your pussy away from that cat," Ransom went on. "Not all demons are created alike."

"Does Chess really lose all his powers when he has sex?" I asked. My mind was still reeling from the thought that I might've put my attentive, thoughtful Cheshire Cat in danger.

Callister and Ransom both nodded.

"I know you saw it happen firsthand," said Callister as Ransom unlocked the door. "And you know I'm right."

We stepped into a long black hallway, lit only by torches mounted to the walls. I had no idea where we were headed, but my wrists were bound and I was wearing a leash.

I went where I was told.

"Stay here," Ransom said to me. "I'll be right back."

A metal claw reached out of the wall and made a fist around the handle of my leash. Then Ransom disappeared.

Speaking of things disappearing, some of the loathing towards me had disappeared from Callister's face. He was back to being a tattooed bad boy with a bright teal pompadour. I still didn't like him, but I hated him less now than I did five minutes ago.

He actually cared about his friends.

Still, something wasn't quite adding up.

"Hey, Callister? If I wasn't safe with a demon, why did you bring me to another one?"

Callister gave an unconcerned shrug.

"It's like Ransom said earlier . . . not all demons are created alike. Chess is a Cheshire Cat. Ransom is an incubus."

I rolled my eyes at him.

"Yeah, I didn't exactly study the different categories of demons when I was in school. What's an incubus?"

Callister stifled a laugh. His eyes crinkled at the corners, and for the first time since I'd met him, I saw a smile spread across his face.

It was genuine.

I never said it was sweet.

"C'mon, Callister," I whined while tugging feebly at the leash. The claw holding the other end wasn't going to let go. "What's an incubus?"

He shook his head, still holding back a laugh.

"Oh Alice . . . you naive little fool. You're about to find out."

CHAPTER
TWO

RANSOM

I breathed a sigh of relief, knowing that nobody in Wonderland would be able to find the Vorpal Sword. I'd hidden it well. Much better than Hatter, although he'd done a fine job keeping it hidden from the Red Queen all these years.

If that psychotic harpy ever found it, there was no saving our realm.

We would all be doomed.

The snap of the door closing behind me echoed against the walls as I walked through yet another portal into the hallway outside my private quarters.

I still could hardly believe that Alice was finally here, although I understood why Callister was so frustrated.

She'd certainly taken her fucking time.

She'd taken so long that I'd almost written her off as a pipe dream. I'd watched alongside everyone in Wonderland as our realm sank further into rot and ruin and despair.

But now that Alice was here . . .

My, my . . . how she'd grown.

Firm tits . . . round ass . . . little waist . . . supple curves that all but begged to be tied up, squeezed, slapped, and spanked.

And such a surly, pouting mouth. I had no doubt that before long, those lips would find as much pleasure in sucking my cock as they did by insulting me.

Breaking this brat was going to be so much fun.

She was still kneeling where I'd left her, her delicate wrists cuffed behind her back. The leather leash and collar were so perfectly draped around her elegant neck and between her firm tits. Anger rolled off her in waves, her eyes narrowed into slits beneath the bunny mask.

Her pout twisted into a sneer the moment she saw me.

"Took you long enough," she snapped, her tone biting. "Did you actually go to Hell?"

I strode across the marble floor, the silk of my robe whispering around my bare legs, and crouched before her. A gold rubber ball gag with black leather straps materialized in front of her face.

"Watch your tone, or I'll stuff this into that pretty mouth of yours."

Alice's nostrils flared, but she held her tongue.

Smart girl.

I rose and waved a hand. The ball gag fell to the floor and shattered into a glittering cloud of dust. Meanwhile, an ornate door shimmered into existence. Alice's eyes widened in surprise.

"How did you do that?" she asked.

"I used my dazzling imagination," I replied dryly, grasping her leash. "Now come along, bunny."

"Where are we going? The hallway didn't lead here before."

"The Rabbit Hole has many secret tunnels," I explained. "We're continuously building in shortcuts and alternate routes for security. If you don't know how to access them, you'll be hopelessly lost."

18

I let the implied threat hang in the air. Deep down, Alice was a clever girl; she'd catch my meaning.

Don't even try to escape.

"Come." I walked through, the leash in my hand pulling taut until my newest bunny scrambled from her knees to follow me.

"What are you planning to do in here?" she asked, peering around at the opulent bathroom as I led her inside.

She glanced around in wonder at a giant mirror that reflected the gold fixtures, the black marble countertops, and a sunken tub full of steam and opalescent bubbles. It was big enough for a dozen people.

I do enjoy group activities.

"You have questions, I have answers," I said, stopping beside the edge of the sunken tub. With a flick of my wrist, the mask and cuffs fell away, clattering to the floor.

I left her leash and collar on.

More control that way.

Alice gathered two handfuls of her messy hair, modestly draping it over her tits before eyeing me warily. I didn't mind. Thanks to the giant mirror, I had a perfect view of her gorgeous ass.

"How about sharing some of those answers? Are you going to tell me what the hell is going on here?"

"Let's get you cleaned up first." I shrugged off my robe and hung it on a nearby hook, watching in satisfaction as Alice's eyes widened at the sight of my naked body.

She certainly seemed to like what she saw.

Good.

My natural allure was already working on her, even if she was consciously resisting it.

I stepped into the tub, the hot water lapping at my ankles, my shins, then my thighs, until I was waist-deep. The leash went taut the further I went into the water.

"Get in here, pet. We have much to discuss."

Alice stared at me, her eyes stormy, before she sighed and stepped into the water. It seemed my naughty little bunny was already learning how to pick her battles.

This was going to be an interesting partnership, indeed.

She slid into the tub across from me, sinking into the bubbles with a groan. "This is pretty nice, I'll give you that much."

"Oh, you'll give me more than that."

My gaze raked over her body, taking in the supple curves and softness of her flesh. Desire stirred within me, as it always does in the presence of an attractive person, but I tamped it down. There would be time enough for that later.

"You think so?" she scoffed.

"I know so."

"Are you suggesting that I actually have a choice in what happens here?"

"Why wouldn't you have a choice?"

Alice rolled her eyes at me—a gesture I found equally endearing as infuriating. Demon heat roiled underneath my skin. Her tone was sarcastic and haughty, and normally I'd have punished her for it, but I let it slide.

It was her first day.

"I dunno—maybe it's hard to believe I have a choice in any of this because you said I'm your prisoner."

"Prisoner . . . pet . . . it's merely semantics." I waved a hand, dismissing her argument. "I've agreed to be your caretaker because you have an essential role to play in the fate of Wonderland. A role only you can fulfill."

"Finding the Vorpal Sword?" She tossed her hair and shot me a smug, arrogant look. "Yeah, I already found it. What did you do with it?"

"Unimportant," I replied with a vague smile. "Finding the sword was simply the first step of your very long journey. Now you must learn what it takes to defeat the Red Queen's Jabberwocky. No one else can slay it but *you*. And you have to use the Vorpal Sword."

"Cool story, bro. You're not telling me anything I don't already know." She crossed her arms over her chest. I watched as her long blonde hair clung to her wet tits, going almost transparent in the water.

"That was the plan from the second I showed up in Wonderland. I was supposed to go to the White Queen's castle and train with the White Knight, but obviously you decided you had a better plan."

"I *do* have a better plan. Obviously."

"Well? What is it?"

"It's not all that different from your original plan."

Alice arched a brow at me, not bothering to hide her scowl. "Then why the fuck did you drag me here?"

"You weren't dragged," I corrected. "You were carried."

"Dragged . . . carried . . . it's just semantics," she mocked.

I narrowed my eyes at her.

Such fire.

Such insolence.

It took everything I had not to grab Alice by the collar and fuck the sneer off her lips. My demon blood began to simmer with arousal.

First day or not, she was definitely going to get herself punished again before the day was done. She had no idea what she was in for.

I couldn't wait.

"What makes you think you'll be any better at training me than the White Knight?" she demanded.

"I'll be the first to tell you that the White Knight is the best sword fighter in all of Wonderland," I explained, still imagining how her lips would look stretched around my cock. "Unfortunately, you'll need more education than he alone can provide."

I leaned forward, pinning her with my gaze as I coiled the

extra slack of her leash around my hand. I'd learned the hard way that if you give a brat an inch, they'll take a kingdom.

"You've seen but a fraction of the horrors in this place. Did Chess and Hatter explain to you that Wonderland goes through seasons of tyrannical Red Queens and her Jabber-wockies?"

"Yeah."

"And did they tell you that it's always a different Alice who come to save us?"

"Yeah. It doesn't make sense why it has to be an Alice, but whatever."

"There are many complications from you arriving as a grown woman rather than a child," I continued. My gaze drifted down to her breasts, which were floating in the water, before returning to look her in the eye.

"One of those complications is the fact that the Red Queen has had all that extra time to become more powerful. She's more wicked and more evil than ever before in the history of Wonder-land. The Jabberwocky is a demonic representation of all the darkness in her heart. And now that demon is larger and more terrifying than it's ever been."

Intrigued by this, Alice tilted her head to one side. "How do I know if you're lying?"

"I can show you what the Red Queen's evil looks like in its current form, if you wish." I waved my hand through the air, summoning an image out of the giant mirror across the room.

The balmy air around us shimmered as scenes of suffering appeared.

Subjects of the Red Queen, abused and oppressed.

An old woman beaten for not working fast enough.

A child's body dangling from the gallows, his only crime was stealing bread to feed his bedridden grandfather.

Villages were burned and pillaged by the Queen's soldiers.

Alice watched in disbelief as the scenes of suffering shifted to public executions. Nobles and commoners alike were beheaded on the Queen's order for the most minor of offenses.

An elderly lord came to court in a pair of shoes she didn't like.

A young handmaiden giggled too loudly.

Their heads rolled as the crowd screamed.

The final vision showed a man—the Red King, placing a rose on his wife's bedside table. The Red Queen flew into a full-on rage as she realized her precious morning rose was not red, but a bright shade of pink.

A shriek tore from Alice's throat as an enormous dragon-like creature materialized in front of the king, roaring and snapping its powerful jaws.

The Jabberwocky.

It leapt out of the Red Queen's chest and lashed out at the king. His limbs were ripped off one by one, until finally his shrieking head was eaten. His body disappeared in seconds. Only a thick puddle of red remained on the rug where he'd once stood.

All because he'd given the Red Queen the wrong color rose.

Then the Jabberwocky turned to us.

Venom-laced saliva dripped from rows of razor-sharp teeth, its eyes glowing red with uncontrolled rage and bloodlust.

Claws scraped against the bathroom tiles as it charged straight for me and Alice, who now cowered behind me, clinging to me for protection. I dispelled the illusion just before the monster attacked, leaving her trembling in the aftermath.

I glanced over my shoulder at her terrified expression.

"Still think I'm lying?" I asked softly.

She swallowed hard and shook her head before letting go of me.

"Good. Believe it or not, Alice, I'm trying to help you save Wonderland. The Red Queen is a monster. Her Jabberwocky will tear you to shreds without the proper skills and knowledge to face it. The Vorpal Sword must be used for the death

23

blow . . . but as you can see, you aren't going to simply walk up to a demon like that and pierce its heart. You need training beyond how to wield a sword. You'll need mental fortitude, endurance, and patience. You'll need to know how to lead an army."

Alice blinked in stunned silence.

"I don't have what it takes to deal with . . . with *that*!"

"I know," I replied grimly. "But with the right training, you will."

She looked up at me, eyes dark with worry. "If I kill the Jabberwocky, will it make the queen weaker?"

"Yes. Perhaps it will even open a path to remove her from power entirely." I lifted Alice's chin, chiding myself for nearly giving away the plan Callister and I had come up with. Alice didn't need to know everything. Not yet. "You want to help these poor people of Wonderland, don't you, bunny?"

She nodded hesitantly.

"That's my good little pet." I smiled, letting my thumb brush over her lower lip. "Keep it up, and you'll be trained in no time."

Alice gave an obedient, understanding nod.

"When do we start training?"

My mouth curled into a knowing grin. I jiggled the leash enough for her to feel it move against her collar.

"We've already begun. So far, I'm unimpressed with what you know. But you'll learn."

I conjured a soft sea sponge and a bar of soap, placing them on the water's edge.

"You reek of Chess and Hatter." I shook my head in disapproval. "I won't have their scent lingering all over my pet bunny while she's in training. Wash it off."

"I thought those guys were your friends," she replied, eyeing me suspiciously.

"They are."

"I thought you didn't care if I fucked them."

"I don't," I explained with a seductive grin. "However, this is *my* club, and while you're here, you are *my* pet. I decide *when* my bunny gets to fuck . . . *where* she gets fucked . . . *who* she gets to fuck . . . and *how* she gets fucked . . . "

A blush stained her cheeks as she looked away.

"I'm not your bunny."

I lunged across the tub and grabbed her chin, forcing her to meet my gaze. "You are whatever I choose to make you!" My fingers tightened, almost bruising the delicate skin. "Right now you're weak. Shallow. Irresponsible. Self-centered. Severely lacking in discipline. I'm going to change *all* of that. Even if I have to break you first."

She tried to jerk her head away but I held her fast.

I realized in that moment, this brat wasn't going to break so easily.

But when it happened, she would shatter.

The sooner, the better.

I stood up to my full height and gripped the leash tighter, reveling in the fear blooming in Alice's eyes as my true demonic form emerged. My horns lengthened, curving back over my skull, and my leathery black wings unfurled behind me, splashing our bodies with warm water.

"You have no name unless we're alone. You will not speak my name *ever*. You will call me your king. You will do everything I say without hesitation. You may ask questions, although you are not entitled to answers. In return, I'll transform you into the warrior you need to be to slay the Jabberwocky and stop the Red Queen. Refuse, and their evil sickness will consume every person, every creature, and every living thing until Wonderland is nothing but ash and bone. The choice is yours."

I continued to hold Alice's chin in my hand, letting my words fully sink in. It was an impossible choice, but it was still a choice.

Whether she wished it or not, she seemed to understand that her fate was in my hands now. As much as I wanted to see her become the champion who would save us all, her submission would be the ultimate prize.

"Wash yourself. Rid yourself of every trace of Chess and Hatter."

Alice flinched at my wings, at my horns, at my size, but her gaze didn't waver. Instead, she fumbled for the soap and the sponge, her hands trembling as she worked up a thick lather.

The scent of jasmine filled the air, bubbles sliding over her skin. I imagined them to be my seed, marking her as mine. She slid the sponge over her collarbone and between her breasts.

"No. Start at your cunt. I'd like to see firsthand what condition my friends left it in."

Her cheeks flushed but she obeyed, sliding the sponge over the soft folds between her legs.

"Spread your knees apart so I can see."

She looked up and frowned.

"How exactly is this helping save Wonderland?"

I smirked at her. "You need to learn how to take orders. How can I put my faith in you on the battlefield when you won't even wash your filthy cunt in front of me?"

She immediately bit her lip, her curious gaze trailing over my horns and wings as I shook my head.

"What did I tell you about biting your lip?"

"That it's your job," she murmured.

I hummed in pleasure.

"That's right. Now apologize."

"I'm sorry."

I gave her leash a sharp tug.

"Address me properly when you apologize to me."

She narrowed her eyes, her chin jutting out in defiance. Her lips were too pursed to bite them, and I knew she was considering a bratty retort.

Three.

Two.

One.

"Is your ego really that fragile?"

I didn't answer with words. I answered by lifting her out of the water and up on a cushion that had a round frame built all around it. I attached the leather cuffs around her wrists to clips on the upper edges of the frame, then conjured leather cuffs just below her knees.

Alice's legs thrashed in the water as I attached one knee to the frame, then the other, leaving her pussy spread wide open for me. With a wave of my hand I tilted back the chair to get a perfect view of her sex. Partially hidden behind white foamy lather were beautiful pink folds that beckoned for a caress.

I longed to give her one with my tongue.

Too bad she'd been so naughty.

"Apologize properly."

"Fuck you!" she yelled.

It only made me chuckle.

"You haven't earned that privilege," I told her, closing the distance between us in one step. I brought my face close to hers, our noses touching. I smiled, a predatory glint in my eyes. "Not yet . . . but you will. Before long, you'll be begging for my cock, desperate for me to fuck you."

Alice shook her head in denial, but doubt flickered across her face. She had no idea what she was in for with me. But she'd learn soon enough.

Oh this was going to be fun, breaking that fiery spirit of hers. I could already feel my cock hardening at the thought. My lips twisted into a wicked smirk as I feasted my eyes on the sight before me—Alice's body trussed up in restraints, her most sensitive flesh exposed and vulnerable.

I basked in the knowledge that I had her right where I wanted her.

She was completely at my mercy.

The flick of my finger activated the jets surrounding us and I

27

sent a gentle arc of warm water cascading onto her clit. A sharp gasp escaped her lips as her body went taut with sensation. She thrashed wildly in an effort to free herself from her restraints, but to no avail. The only thing she could do now was succumb to my will.

My demonic powers were at full force as I directed streams of hot water from multiple jets onto Alice's clit while she gasped and writhed in pleasure, begging for relief. Every time she got close to the edge of orgasm, I turned off the water, prolonging her suffering with my relentless teasing.

The deeper she ached for me, the harder she throbbed, the more it fed me.

Fueled me.

Satisfied me.

Each time she was almost at her peak I savored the moment, stretching out her suffering before mercilessly flooding her with hot water and restrained pleasure again and again. I could feel my own passion rising as her anguished cries filled the room, bouncing off the walls and intensifying around us both.

I reached down and caressed my shaft in rhythm to the pulses of water that teased her clit. I was getting harder with each passing second. My fingers moved faster and faster as I stroked my length, the pleasure of it almost too much to bear.

I wanted to take her now, to make her mine.

I wanted to sink into that velvet heat and make her come undone all over my cock.

But I wanted her to *beg* for it.

I knew that day would come soon.

For now, I had other plans.

Wonderland's champion was spoiled. Entitled. She needed to learn that victories could be taken away at the very last second.

Alice's body was quivering with need, and I reveled in having her at my mercy. Every unsatisfied moan, every pitiful whimper she uttered was feeding my power, strengthening my resolve.

She wanted so badly to come, and I wasn't going to let her. I wanted to make her anguish last forever.

"Do you want me to lick you?" I asked, only half-serious.

"Yeah!" she gasped. "I mean, yes, my king!"

I chuckled as I watched Alice shaking and panting like a bitch in heat. Her eyes were wide and her body was trembling with longing. She'd remembered her manners, so I ran my hands over her soft thighs, feeling her shiver beneath my touch.

My lips moved across her neck, tasting her sweetness, and my tongue snaked its way down her body. She moaned in pleasure as I teased her nipples, sucking and biting before making my way down her belly. I could feel her desire growing with each movement of my tongue as I made my way between her legs.

Finally I kneeled down in front of her, my mouth just inches from her wet pussy. Heat rose off her body, the scent of her arousal filling my senses, the slick sheen of it daring me to mount her in a single thrust.

Somehow, I resisted the urge.

I ran my tongue along her slit, teasing it apart with soft strokes, and then licked with broad laps like a lazy hound. My tongue flickered and fluttered before my mouth settled in place and gently sucked on her swollen nub.

Her tangy sweetness flooded into my mouth, tempting my brain, beckoning, "*drink me.*"

Alice tipped her head back and moaned with abandon. The second her hips rocked against my mouth I pulled myself away.

"Noooo!" she wailed in protest. "Why did you stop?"

"I already told you . . . I decide *when* my bunny gets to fuck . . . *where* she gets fucked . . . *who* she gets to fuck . . . and *how* she gets fucked . . . " I licked my lips, then raised a brow at her. "And I distinctly recall you saying that you weren't my bunny."

Alice glowered at me, lips pouting, her jaw feathering.

"Yeah, well . . . you said I'm whatever you choose to make me . . . *my king*. So I guess I'm your bunny."

A low growl of approval rolled up inside of me.

It took all I had not to sink balls deep into her sweet, slick pussy.

I took a deep breath and gave her a faint smile.

"Such good manners, my pet. And such a good memory, too. I suppose I should probably let you come." My mouth drifted back down to her slit, and I sucked and licked her until her until the brink of orgasm. "But I'm not going to."

"You fucking asshole!" she howled while thrashing in her restraints. "I'm sorry, my king. Please—don't stop!"

Her sexual energy was radiating out of every pore of her skin, funneling into mine, coursing through my body. I lived for moments like this.

"Do you want me to fuck you?" I casually asked, still stroking my cock.

Eyeing the size of my shaft, she nodded cautiously, then bit down on her lip.

"Tell me, Alice . . . what did I say about biting your lip?"

She glared at me for a moment, but being restrained and spread wide made her realize how vulnerable she truly was in my presence.

"It's your job . . . my king."

I let out a sigh of delight.

"You're learning very quickly, bunny. I'm so proud of you."

I leaned forward and let my teeth graze against her bottom lip, nipping gently before slipping my tongue into her mouth. As I kissed her, I brought the tip of my cock to her pussy, stroking up and down the wet slit, rubbing it against her swollen clit with agonizingly slow movements.

She bleated out a little groan of anticipation into my kiss, her hips bucking against the leather straps holding her in place. I knew she was aching for me to fill her, to stretch her with my inhuman shape.

Feeling her body contort in response to my touch sent cascades of pleasure coursing through my veins. I could feel every shudder and moan vibrate against my chest. The intoxicating scent of our shared arousal filled each breath I took as I kissed her again and again. Her moans grew louder with every caress of my cock against her clit, begging for me to slip inside and soothe her throbbing core.

But like I told her earlier . . . she hadn't earned that privilege.

Breaking the kiss, I took my cock away from her and snapped my fingers.

The water drained in seconds, and suddenly the tub was a pit filled with soft cushions.

I snapped my fingers again.

My bad bunny was now wearing her black leather mask.

"I'm afraid I don't trust you enough with that vicious tongue of yours," I said as the ball gag reappeared in my hands.

"What the fuck? Noooo!" she whined.

Ignoring her protests, I coaxed the golden sphere past Alice's teeth and buckled it in place just as a masked trio of my best bunnies in training appeared.

"Yes, my king?" the shortest one asked as he stepped to the edge of the tub.

"My new pet needs to learn some manners," I explained, and motioned to Alice. "Cage her and take her downstairs. Show her what she's in for. And use a spreader bar. I don't want her coming until I give permission."

I glanced at the tallest bunny, one of my personal favorites. "You can stay here."

"Thank you, my king," he replied with a polite bow.

So well-trained.

Alice was torn between watching the two bunnies who were

taking her off the frame, and watching the third one slip off his robe and crawl across the cushions towards me.

Alice's eyes were practically bulging out of her head with a potent mix of arousal and unbearable frustration as I was descended upon by a masculine work of art.

I lay back and reveled in the ecstasy as my favorite toy entertained me. His tongue explored my aroused flesh, tasting my body from head to toe. Meanwhile, my eyes never left Alice's.

I'd seen envy and resentment plenty of times, although I'm not sure that Alice had ever experienced it to this degree. She didn't put up much of a fight as the bunnies secured her hands behind her back.

Meanwhile, my beautiful, black-haired bunny was devouring my cock with his greedy, hungry mouth while his hands worshipped my nipples and balls. I needed Alice to understand that I wasn't just an incubus—I was a *king*!

If she wanted my cock, my climax, she'd have to fucking *earn* it. Competition among my bad little bunnies was going to be fierce.

And I couldn't wait for the games to begin.

I admired the juxtaposition of Alice being restrained, unsatisfied, and left wanting, while I throat-fucked a hungry mouth as hard as I pleased. The two bunnies attached a spreader bar to her ankles, keeping her knees apart.

No climax for her.

I, on the other hand, wouldn't last much longer.

While I ran my fingers through my best bunny's short curls, Alice's arms and legs quivered against the strength of her restraints. She groaned in desperation as she was placed into a cage on wheels, knowing that she'd missed her opportunity to be fucked with ruthless abandon.

With every thrust I made into that hot, welcoming mouth, I felt my body tense up, inching closer and closer to orgasm.

Poor Alice was hoisted up by the other two bunnies,

watching with envy as I writhed beneath my lover in raw, carnal delight.

"Remember what I said," I panted. "Don't let anything touch her pussy without my permission! I licked it, so it's *mine!*"

"Of course, my king," they replied in unison.

I turned my attention back to the handsome young man bobbing up and down on my glistening cock.

"And you . . . "

He lifted his head, such devotion in his eyes.

"Yes, my king?"

My body began to shake uncontrollably as intense euphoria coursed through me. I thrust deep into his mouth, then erupted in an uncontrollable explosion, showering the back of his throat with my scorching release.

"Drink me."

CHAPTER
THREE

CHESS

The rotting remains of the Wickedwood Forest loomed before us as Hatter and I made our way along the overgrown path. The sickly-sweet stench of decay hung heavy in the air, as if the very essence of Wonderland was rotting from within.

Probably because that's exactly what was happening.

Gone were the whimsical nonsense creatures I was used to seeing . . . creatures that existed simply to prove that someone had imagined them. Gone were the bright colors, the bizarre yet wondrous logic that defined Wonderland.

Now there was only decay.

What was once a whimsical and colorful realm had turned into a festering wasteland under the tyrannical rule of the Red Queen. Ruin and rot tainted everything her madness touched.

My demonic nature always felt more comfortable in the cycles of darkness over the centuries, but I craved the light that Alice had brought into my world. Without her, Wonderland was bleak and colorless.

I needed to find her again.

So did Hatter.

So did all of Wonderland.

I prayed that she was still alive. If she wasn't . . .

I couldn't let myself go there.

I longed to return to the carefree days before the queen's reign of terror, back when Callister and I could laugh with Hatter for hours on end, sipping tea and playing ridiculous games that had no rules or winners.

All that mattered was pleasure . . . and Hatter knew how to throw a party.

Simply the memory of him being the gracious host soured my mood. We'd been sniping at each other for hours, unable to agree on a plan to find Alice.

I was furious at him for fucking himself to exhaustion and losing track of her. I trusted him, and he'd let me down.

I was even more furious with myself for draining my powers by fucking Alice. If I hadn't been so weak and selfish, I could have protected her from whoever had taken her. Now we had no idea where she'd gone, or if she was even still alive.

"This place reeks of death," Hatter muttered. His boots squished into the mud with every step. I watched in disgust as dark, brackish water seeped over the tops, soaking his feet with the putrid stink of rot. "If you were really my friend, you'd be walking through this festering muck with me, not floating above the ground."

"If you were really my friend, you wouldn't wish that on me," I replied. "Blame your mother for fucking an earthbound fae instead of a Cheshire Cat demon."

"I'd rather be fae than a demon who loses his powers every time he blows a load," Hatter snapped back. "I thought you knew when to stop fucking!"

I sighed, pinching the bridge of my nose between two fingers.

I knew when to stop fucking.

The trouble was that I didn't *want* to stop fucking.

Not when I was fucking Alice.

I wanted—no, I *needed* her to know what it felt like to be drenched in my demon seed. I needed her to know how far she could be stretched to take the full length of my demon cock. To fill her hot, wet, tight little pussy with a veritable flood of my utter devotion until it spilled down her tender thighs.

I'd mounted her.

Ravaged her.

Buried myself in her.

Claimed her.

In the heat of the moment, the temporary loss of my powers seemed a small price to pay. I'd counted on my friend to have my back.

Yet that gamble had cost me dearly.

Serves me right for trusting a madman.

"I *do* know when to stop fucking, Hatter. I shouldn't have let myself—"

"At least you have an excuse for not waking up," Hatter grumbled. "I was just being greedy, fucking her so many times that I rendered myself unconscious."

"I was being greedy as well," I pointed out, grateful for his spark of clarity.

"I was greedier. You came once. I came so many times that—"

"Yes, yes, you don't need to remind me how you're able to fuck as much as you like," I warned him. "The point is, we lost Alice. Where are we even *going*?"

"I don't know!" Hatter finally admitted, throwing up his hands in frustration. "I thought if I walked with enough purpose, we'd find her."

"I don't think that's how walking with purpose works," I grimaced while resisting the urge to strangle my friend.

"Going in circles is more effective than going nowhere," the Mad Hatter rationalized, wagging an accusatory finger at me. "Although, the joy lies not in the destination, but in the maddening journey itself. All we can do is twist and twirl and dance to the chaos. *That*, my dear Cheshire Cat, is the essence of life's wicked game. Going nowhere—stagnation—is the true curse that stifles the soul."

My heart sank as I recognized the telltale signs of my friend teetering on the edge of madness. I loved Hatter like a brother, and I appreciated his unique and colorful perspectives on life.

But his timing was terrible.

I needed him to hang onto his lucidity long enough to find Alice and get to the White Queen's court before her wicked older sister beat us to it.

"Perhaps we should go back and search again for clues?" I suggested halfheartedly. We'd already scoured the garden repeatedly and found nothing. We had no clues, no leads, and no idea where Alice had disappeared to.

"As long as we're walking, that's all that matters." Hatter shook his head so hard that his top hat teetered back and forth on his head. "Alice will turn up. She always does. We need to keep walking so we can find her before the Red Queen gets her hands on her."

My fists clenched at the thought of The Red Queen torturing Alice the way she had tortured Hatter back when he stole the Vorpal Sword. He'd been burned and flayed and beaten within an inch of his life.

The poor fae was too insane to know day from night, let alone the location of a priceless weapon he'd hidden in a fit of lunacy. The Red Queen was so enraged that she wanted to cut off his head, but he was the only person in Wonderland who knew where the Vorpal Sword was.

I would rip out the Queen's black heart with my own claws before I let her touch Alice.

"We'll find her," I said, as much to reassure myself as Hatter. "Somehow, we'll find her. She's the only light left in this rotten world. We *have* to find her."

I couldn't give up on her.

Alice was out there somewhere, and we would scour every inch of our ruined Wonderland to find her . . .

Unless Hatter and I got ourselves killed in the process.

I was starting to feel it might end up that way. Hatter was starting to lose his mind, and I was still woefully powerless.

"You'll regain your powers faster if you stop trying to read my mind," he said, cutting through my inner thoughts.

I bristled at his uncanny fae senses catching me out. He had the ears of a wolf and the eyes of a hawk, but he had the brains of a grimsnatch. They were wiry, clever creatures, yet easily distracted by shiny objects.

"My powers are coming back just fine, thank you very much."

Hatter shot me a wild, slightly maniacal grin. His blue eye sparkled bright with excitement while his dark one remained solemn and sane.

"Is that so? Then when were you going to tell me that we're being followed?"

I scowled at him.

"What are you talking about? My demon sense of hearing is better than any fae—even yours. I would know if we were being followed."

"You wouldn't know shit until it was too late," said a familiar mocking voice from behind us. Unable to invert my body as I normally might've done, I physically turned around to see Callister leaning against a gnarled tree.

His lean, sinewy figure was enveloped in a cloud of blue smoke as he puffed away on a blackberry cigarette. The sweet aroma of his magic tobacco wafted through the sharp, festering air, giving our noses a welcome reprieve.

However, the smug expression on his face made my fingers itch with the urge to punch him in his tattooed throat.

The bastard knew something, I was sure of it, but getting information out of him would be like pulling teeth.

I'd tried before.

It didn't work.

Not on a masochist like Callister.

He enjoyed the pain. Reveled in it.

"What remarkable timing you have," said Hatter, unable to hide the suspicious gaze beneath the brim of his top hat.

"Yes, curiouser and curiouser," I said, equally suspicious. "Where is she, Callister?"

"Who?"

"You *know* who."

"Alice? How should I know?" he replied with a careless shrug. "I haven't seen her since your last tea party. Good riddance, I say."

I narrowed my eyes at him. Callister had never believed in this Alice's ability to defeat the Red Queen, despite the long-standing tradition that only an Alice could be the one to save Wonderland.

From the moment he laid eyes on her, Callister had made it clear that he thought this Alice was too spoiled and selfish to be our champion. He thought her imagination was too dim and dull to outwit our evil queen.

"You're lying," I accused.

"Am I?" He raised a brow, staring me down with unrepentant eyes. "Or are you simply too blinded by your affection for the girl to see the truth?"

"The truth is you've never given her a chance!" Hatter snapped.

"I *did* give her a chance, which is more than she deserved," Callister countered. "Your precious Alice might be good for a fuck, but she is *not* the savior you wish her to be!"

Anger boiled in my veins, nearly choking me with its intensity.

"Enough! She solved Hatter's riddle and found the Vorpal Sword. If you know where Alice is, you will tell us now!"

Callister scoffed, clearly unimpressed by my threat. Without my magic, I was no match for him and we all knew it.

"Or what? You'll glare at me until I expire of boredom?" He took a long drag on his cigarette, regarding us with contempt. "Face it, Chess—the little slut got bored and went home. Best accept it and move on."

"I will never accept that," I ground out. "If Alice got bored, she wouldn't have taken the Vorpal Sword with her! She *can't* take it with her. The sword can't leave Wonderland. She's out there somewhere, and I won't stop looking until I find her—with or without your help!"

Callister's lips curled into a sneer, clearly enjoying my frustration.

"Then you're as foolish as you are powerless, Chess. By all means, continue your wild goose chase. Even if you find her and the sword, that little whore won't last two seconds against the queen," Callister said. "Might as well save yourselves the trouble and focus your efforts elsewhere."

I stared at the space where he stood, anger and resentment warring inside me. The cloud of blue smoke continued to swirl and creep through the space between us, until the sweet, soft scent filled my nose. I let out a slow breath, reigning in my turbulent emotions.

"Where else would we focus our efforts? Alice is supposed to be the one to save Wonderland . . . but it sounds like you have other plans."

Something in Callister's face shifted, and I knew that even without the full power of my magic, I'd picked up on his deepest desires.

The woods around us had gone eerily silent, as if the creatures were holding their breath in anticipation of what came next. An owl hooted softly in the distance, the lonely sound piercing the quiet.

"I *do* have plans," Callister finally said. He dropped the butt of his cigarette to the ground, his eyes crinkling in satisfaction as the embers hissed in the wet, moldy sludge below. "The only question is if you two have the stomach for what needs to be done."

"I can't read your thoughts," I confessed.

"I can," Hatter said quietly, grim sobriety etched into every line of his face. "He doesn't want to waste time finding Alice or training her how to use the Vorpal Sword. He doesn't want to waste energy fighting the Red Queen's army or her Jabberwocky. He wants us to cut out the source of all this rot and destroy it once and for all."

I sighed, raking a hand through my hair. "How do we defeat the Red Queen without Alice or the Vorpal Sword? She'll never give up her throne willingly."

"Perhaps Callister is right, and it's time for a change in dynasty," he said, a dangerous glint in his mismatched eyes. "One that doesn't involve an Alice at all."

I stared at him, then turned to Callister, stunned. "You can't mean—"

"Yes. We kill the bitch," he finished bluntly. "It's the only way, my friend. You know I'm right."

My heart twisted at the thought. However corrupted Wonderland had become, the Red Queen was still a queen. To assassinate her would be a deplorable act of treason.

But was her rule truly preferable to the alternative? Wonderland was dying, little by little. There was no balance left between the two sisters. Every day that the Red Queen sat on her throne was another day of death and suffering. How much further could we afford to fall before it was too late?

And were we not already traitors for plotting against her by searching for Alice? By supporting the woman destined to bring about her downfall?

But still . . .

We'd only ever helped our Alices slay the Jabberwocky.

Never the Red Queen. What would happen to our realm if we destroyed the woman who ruled over it? The White Queen was many things, but she was not an effective ruler.

I didn't know the answer. I only knew that the fate of Wonderland hung in the balance, and we were running out of time.

I closed my eyes and took a deep breath, sorting through my jumble of thoughts, wishing that the answer would make itself clear to me.

"If you're having doubts, now would be the time to back out," Callister said, lighting a fresh cigarette.

My eyes flew open to find him watching me expectantly. He sucked in a long drag and exhaled a cloud of orange smoke. It cut through the reeking, fetid stench of rot, filling the air with the scent of tangerines.

"I won't think any less of you if you back out of the plan." He paused to laugh. "I mean, I *will* think less of you, but I won't say it to your face."

Hatter clenched his jaw, his eyes burning with determination.

"I'm in," he said with a stiff nod. "I'd love to be rid of that cunt for what she did to your brother. For what she did to *me!*"

Callister gave a nod of approval before turning back to me, his expression unreadable.

"What's it going to be, Chess? Wonderland is already lost. Has been for years. Killing the queen ourselves is the only way to save our world now."

"It's not the *only* way."

Callister arched a brow. "You have a better plan, then?"

"Yes. We find Alice," I said firmly. "Like we've always done. She's the one destined to defeat the Queen, not us. We have to keep looking for her."

"You're only saying that because you miss fucking her brains out," Callister accused.

I slammed him against a tree, the beast within me surging through my veins. "Watch your tongue, Callister, or I'll rip it out!"

He narrowed his eyes and held my gaze. "No you won't. You're not strong enough."

My hand went to his throat, squeezing. He didn't even flinch. Of course he didn't. A twisted smile played at his lips, and I knew he was enjoying the pain.

"The truth hurts, doesn't it?" he hissed before burning me with his cigarette.

"Stop fighting!" Hatter shouted at us as he tried to pull me off of Callister. "We need to work together if we're going to save Wonderland!"

I let Callister go with a snarl.

"Alice has always been the one to stop the Red Queen. What if murdering the Red Queen throws our entire world out of balance?"

"Have you looked around lately?" Hatter snapped. He straightened his hat and vest and motioned at our surroundings. "The rivers are flowing with pus. Black ooze drips from the trees and covers the forest floor. How much worse does it have to get until you're willing to take matters into your own hands?"

I sighed and gazed out at the ruins of Wonderland. "I just want our home back," I said softly. "Alice is the key. We have to believe she'll return."

"And what if she's already gone?" Hatter countered. "What if she's already vanished back to her own world? How long do you want to wait for her to come back?"

I set my jaw, refusing to consider a Wonderland without Alice. She was my light in the darkness, my glimpse of joy in a bleak world. Wonderland needed her to defeat the Red Queen, but I needed her for reasons that went far deeper. She had brought color back into my life, and without her, everything was shades of gray once more.

"She will return," I said firmly. "She has to."

Callister's lips curled into a grim expression.

"What if she's still here, but she's fallen into the hands of the Red Queen? What's your plan then, Chess?"

I ground my teeth, frustration simmering in my veins. I'd killed soldiers without a second thought, but that was in self-defense. The thought of assassinating our mad queen left a bitter taste in my mouth.

Perhaps I hated the idea because it meant accepting what Wonderland had truly become: a place where fantasy and dreams were rotting away to nothingness.

Hatter placed a hand on my shoulder. "I don't like the idea any more than you do, Chess. But we're running out of time and options. If we don't stop the Red Queen soon—"

He broke off as a distinct, bone-chilling howl split the air.

Fuck.

Abyssal hounds.

Not many sounds in Wonderland scared me, but this one did.

Abyssal hounds were a nightmarish canine creation of the Red Queen's twisted imagination. They were covered with jet-black fur and had eyes that burned with otherworldly, bright red flames. Their fangs and claws were sharp as glass, and they could traverse through shadows, appearing and disappearing at will.

By the time you heard them, it was usually too late to run. And without the full strength of my powers, I was as weak and vulnerable as a Cheshire Kitten.

The Red Queen wanted a word with me, Callister, and Hatter.

And she had sent her hounds to find us.

Callister said nothing, his face an impassive mask as he scanned the trees. But his jaw was tight, shoulders tense. His tattoos writhed, venomous insects and serpents ready to strike.

For a long moment, nothing moved. Not even the insects dared to crawl through the sludge. Then the underbrush rustled and our attackers poured out—the Red Queen's foot soldiers and her demonic abyssal hounds.

So many of them.

Too many.

We were completely surrounded.

Another blood-curdling howl bayed nearby. I whirled around to see half a dozen abyssal hounds emerging from the forest, their red eyes glowing and slavering jaws snapping.

The hounds stalked forward, flanking us on all sides. Callister and Hatter conjured swords into their hands while casting me a grim look. My magic was still drained from my encounter with Alice, leaving me at a huge disadvantage against the fearsome beasts.

This was it. Without my ability to shift into a massive beast, we were done for. Fear clawed icy fingers down my spine.

Hatter bared his teeth in a savage grin, his bright blue eye pulsing with excitement. "Ready to dance, my friends?"

The abyssal hounds struck first, lunging at us with fanged maws gaping. Unable to disappear at will, I dodged left, barely avoiding the snap of razor-sharp teeth. The hound's hot, fetid breath washed over me as it sailed past.

Callister was there in an instant, his sword flashing. The hound's head tumbled free in a spray of black blood. The body crumpled, already dissolving into acrid smoke.

"One down!" Callister yelled.

All around us the fight raged. Hatter wove and spun around me, his blade singing as it carved through one opponent after another. Body parts littered the forest floor. A foot here, a furry leg there.

But still, they kept coming.

A soldier's sword caught me across the ribs and I gasped at the sudden blaze of pain. My shirt and jacket grew wet with blood. The soldier raised his sword for a powerful blow. I scrambled back, my boot heel catching on a root.

46

Then Hatter was there, his sword cleaving through my attacker's torso in a single vicious swipe. Blood and gore splattered us both.

"Chess! Are you alright?" he cried.

I nodded weakly. Hatter whirled back to the fight, green coat flying. His eyes were feverish, teeth bared in a snarl. He had never looked more dangerous or deadly.

Callister lunged at the nearest abyssal hound, slicing his sword through the air. The hound dodged and snapped at his arm, ignoring the biting snakes as it ripped through fabric and flesh. Callister cursed, blood dripping down his arm, but he held his ground.

Two hounds rushed at Hatter, who swung his sword in a wide arc, beheading one in a spray of black blood. The other hound leapt onto his back, claws digging in as it snarled and snapped at his neck. Hatter staggered under the weight and fell to his hands and knees, struggling to reach the hound.

We were tiring.

The wounds were piling up.

But the Red Queen's forces seemed endless.

The abyssal hound's jaws closed around Hatter's leg and he screamed as it shook him like a rag doll. I scrambled for a rock, anything to strike at the beast with, but my hands grasped only dirt.

Before I could react, a pair of gloved hands seized me, wrenching my arms behind my back. I thrashed wildly but the soldier held me fast. More hands grabbed at Callister and Hatter, dragging them down even as they fought against their captors.

It was over in seconds. We were captured.

We had survived, but only just. The Red Queen's message was clear—she wanted us alive, but not without a little taste of her wrath first.

"The three of you are under arrest for harboring a fugitive of

47

Wonderland," one of the soldiers announced. "The penalty for hiding an Alice is death by beheading."

My first instinct was to argue against the charges and deny the accusations, but I'd brought Alice to Hatter's tea party. Callister had dueled with her in front of all the other guests. Hatter had fucked her right on the table.

Someone from that tea party had betrayed us.

Perhaps more than one person.

To try and pretend that none of us had seen Alice would be a surefire way to enrage the queen. And since I had no intention of losing my head, let alone watching it happen to my dearest friends, I said nothing.

I hated myself for it, but I was in no position to fight.

The soldiers bound our wrists and forced us to our feet. Callister swayed, his unique shade of violet blood running from his temple. Hatter leaned heavily on his uninjured leg, his face white with pain. That brilliant blue eye of his was dull and colorless.

If my friends were in this bad of shape, I could only imagine how I appeared to them.

Without another word, the soldiers prodded us forward. We set off through the trees, the path lit by the soldiers' flickering torches. The hounds flanked us, snapping their jaws if any of us slowed down too much.

The terrain grew rockier as we traveled. Jagged cliffs reared up around us, closing in like the walls of a prison. Lightning forked across the bruise-colored sky, thunder rumbling. The first fat drops of rain spattered down.

Before long the rain was falling in sheets, drenching us in seconds. Our shoes slipped on the muddy trail. A soldier clubbed Hatter with the pommel of his sword when he stumbled.

"Keep walking, scum," the soldier growled.

Hatter spit blood but kept moving. His eyes found mine, full of rage and despair.

We crested a rise, and there it was. The Red Queen's castle, anchored in the most advantageous location in the Kingdom of Hearts and Roses.

It loomed before us, a hulking shadow against the stormy sky. Twisted spires clawed at the clouds, while parapets and battlements brooded like hunched-over gargoyles. Banners bearing the Queen's crimson crest snapped in the rising wind.

Lightning flashed, throwing the castle into stark relief. In that instant, I saw the true menace of the place—the iron spikes adorning the gates, the razor-wire coiling atop the walls, the spear-tips of the guards patrolling the ramparts.

The decapitated heads on spikes to remind us of what it meant to displease Her Majesty.

As if there was anything majestic about the diseased cunt who ruled over us all.

The guards pushed us through the gates, across a courtyard slick with slime and rain. Our steps echoed off the imposing stone walls. Torches sputtered in the wind, casting wavering shadows all around us.

We were prodded down a spiral stone staircase, deeper and deeper into the bowels of the castle. The air grew dank, heavy with mold.

Once we arrived at the base of the stairs, the dungeons sprawled out like eight rows of spider legs. Stone cells lined both sides of eight long corridors, with heavy bars caging the wretched inhabitants within. Some peered out at us with sunken, hopeless eyes as we passed by them. Most simply hunched on the floor, despondent.

These were broken souls, crushed by the Queen's iron fist. How long before we shared their fate?

The guards opened a cell and threw us inside. We hit the floor hard, the breath knocked from our lungs. Before we could react, the door clanged shut, locking us in.

"Hope you like it down here, because you're never seeing the light of day again," one guard sneered. His companion laughed.

Their footsteps receded, leaving us in musty gloom. I met Hatter's and Callister's eyes, seeing my own dread reflected in them.

We were the Red Queen's prisoners now.

We were at her mercy.

Unfortunately, she had none to give.

CHAPTER
FOUR

ALICE

My cage rattled faintly over the polished black marble floors, drawing curious glances and outright stares. The sex bunnies in charge of me wore sheer black lingerie and black bunny masks, their coltish legs stretching for miles in seven-inch stiletto heels.

The blue-haired girl on the right stumbled, nearly pulling down my cage. A laugh bubbled up in my throat, muffled by the gag, and she shot me a venomous glare over her shoulder. A glare that clearly said if I didn't choke on my own drool first, she might just arrange an 'accident' for me.

My bare ass scraped against the metal bars of the cage as Trippy and her caramel-haired friend rolled me through the different floors and halls of the Rabbit Hole. Ransom was right about this place—it was a fucking maze. At least the hedge labyrinth had some variation.

Here, the walls all looked the same.

Black, with gold torches.

And doors that apparently appeared and disappeared at will.

Even if I escaped, I'd never find my way out of this place.

Trippy and Caramel—those were their names now, as far as I

was concerned—rolled me along, their mocking laughter contained behind unrestrained hands. They were probably laughing because once upon a time, they'd been exactly where I was right now—tormented and licked and teased to the point that it actually hurt.

My pussy throbbed, swollen and empty. I was so horny that I could've made myself come just by squeezing my thighs together enough, but the spreader bar kept them apart, leaving me exposed.

Maybe I could figure out a way to use this leash hanging from my neck . . .

I tried to imagine the leash floating up and rubbing against my crotch, but it didn't budge. I'd been able to imagine things with Chess and Hatter. I'd changed the color of my dress. I'd conjured a frying pan to fight the Red Queen's soldiers. So why the hell wasn't my imagination working here?

Maybe I was too distracted?

Ransom had edged me for what felt like hours, his hot, slick tongue bringing me to the brink again and again only to stop short, leaving me aching and desperate. I'd been so close when he pulled away, sliding his cock along my clit before thrusting into the mouth of some random bunny boy.

I closed my eyes as I recalled the look on Ransom's gorgeous face when he came. My pussy throbbed at the memory of his voice, his sighs of relief, and heat began pooling low in my belly once more.

It wasn't fair.

That arrogant asshole pissed me off so much, yet somehow he'd made me beg for his tongue and his dick in a matter of hours. When he came down the throat of his favorite boy toy instead of inside me, I nearly sobbed in frustration.

And that cock of his . . .

Holy fucking *shit*! What *was* that?

I thought I'd seen everything the first time I laid eyes on

Chess's demon dong. Ransom's had a similar bulbous texture, wound in a thick cord of muscle that spiraled along the length. It almost looked like two cocks wrapped around each other . . .

But that was impossible.

Wasn't it?

Who the fuck knew? This was Wonderland, a world ruled by imagination . . . and a psycho fae queen. Ransom's entire attitude shifted when he'd mentioned her, making me wonder if there was some kind of beef between them.

I knew that she'd killed the Red King, who happened to be Callister's brother. And Callister and Ransom were friends.

Seemed like enough reason to hate the bitch.

The sensation of drool seeping down my bottom lip pulled me out of my private thoughts. It fell onto the top of my tits as I was wheeled closer to an ornate set of black double doors with a golden rabbit insignia.

Two male sex bunnies grasped the door handles, glancing at me before sharing a look with Trippy and Caramel. I wasn't sure if they were plotting against me or planning to fuck me. Either way, I didn't trust them.

The doors parted, and my jaw would've dropped if there wasn't a fucking gold ball stuffed in my mouth.

My eyes widened, taking in the sight of what could only be The Rabbit Hole.

The opulence hit me like a brick wall. This club was unlike anything I'd ever seen before . . . and I'd been to Ibiza and Monaco multiple times.

This was sin and decadence given form. A temple devoted to lust and desire.

I got the feeling that I was about to become a sacrifice on its altar.

The air was thick with the scent of sex, sweat, and expensive cologne. The walls were covered in black material that looked like crocodile skin, while huge gold chandeliers dripping with crystals hung overhead . . . big enough to swing from.

Every surface was plush black velvet or leather, and gold accents glittered under the warm golden lights. Sex bunnies served drinks and more to eager patrons. The air was alive with laughter, drunken shouts, and moans of ecstasy.

Dealers in lacy corsets expertly shuffled cards at blackjack tables while men ogled their plunging necklines. Black felt baccarat tables and roulette wheels were crowded with gamblers who were either sipping drinks, playing with their stacks of gold chips, or spinning wheels with abandon.

But it wasn't just gambling here.

My nipples pebbled as I took in the sights and sounds. The smacks of hands on flesh, the rattle of chips and dice, the sounds of moans and cries of pleasure and pain. Everything here was a spectacle, meant to entice and arouse.

Male and female dancers gyrated on different platforms and in cages strategically placed to allow for the most visibility, all of them writhing to a slow, sensual bass beat. Some of them were swinging on poles, grinding against the gleaming gold metal.

My gaze swept over a particularly enthusiastic threesome fucking on one of the stages. A male sex bunny was fucking a woman from behind while getting fucked by another man from behind.

A woman was strapped to a St. Andrew's cross, back arching as a man whipped her with a flogger. Another woman had her face buried in a bunny's pussy while she rode a woman with a hot pink strap-on.

My cheeks flamed hot, embarrassment and arousal fighting within me. I wanted to look away but found myself transfixed by the erotic displays of depravity and indulgence playing out.

Another desperate throb pulsed in my clit. The Rabbit Hole was a place of temptation and corruption . . . and exactly what I needed, if I could just get out of this cage and finish what Ransom had started between my legs.

"Like what you see, my pet?" he asked, and I jumped at the seductive tone of his voice.

Speak of the devil . . . or demon.

I peered up at him, pulse skipping. His fingers trailed over the bars of my cage . . . like he couldn't wait to get his hands on me.

He'd changed into a different black suit, this one tailored to emphasize the width of his shoulders. Half of the jacket was covered in gold jacquard tree branches that seemed to be crawling over his body. A black silk shirt was left unbuttoned at the throat, hinting that this was about as casual as he ever looked in public.

But it was his eyes that transfixed me, flecks of gold among the darkness, and full of secrets.

My cage rattled as Trippy and Caramel unlocked the door and swung it open. My head whipped in Ransom's direction so fast that a drop of my drool landed on his elegant golden sleeve. Mortified, all I could do was blink and stare at him as more drool dripped down my chin.

He chuckled, the sound of his laugh rich with amusement.

"Ready to come out and play?"

He crooked a finger at me, a wicked gleam in his eyes. Eager for a taste of freedom, I shuffled to the edge of the cage without a second thought. He reached in and lifted me into his arms, holding me protectively as Caramel removed the spreader bar from my ankles. Then he gently set me down onto the floor, surprising me by how tenderly he handled me.

Gathering my leash in his hands, he led me through the crowd past baccarat tables, roulette wheels and poker games. I watched as money and chips passed hands and I caught glimpses of bodies humping and fucking in shadowy corners. The air was charged with raw sensuality.

All eyes turned our way, gazes heated behind leather masks. People nearby stared openly at us, envy and reverence etched on their faces. Ransom was royalty here, a king holding court.

I shuddered, painfully aware that I was totally out of my depth. Ransom's hand tightened on my leash as we walked, a subtle warning to all:

I belonged to the King of Clubs, and him alone.

Two men in broad red and white striped suits stood on either side of a black velvet rope guarding an ornate private booth. Raised up on a platform, it was obviously the best section in the entire club.

"Good evening, my king," they both said in unison as one of them pulled back the rope and let us in.

"Good evening, Tweedles," he replied, not bothering to introduce us. I knew in that moment, they were the ones who'd taken me from Chess and Hatter.

My heart raced as Ransom led me up the steps and into the heart of his domain. The spacious booth was lavishly furnished with leather couches, velvet cushions, and tables full of flowers, fruit, and expensive liquor.

His warm, strong hand rested on the small of my back, guiding me to the partition that separated him from his guests. It allowed for an unobstructed view of the depraved spectacles on the floor below.

"Look at them," he murmured beside me, "giving in to pleasure, letting go of their inhibitions. People come to The Rabbit Hole to transform into who they were always meant to be." He turned to me, and I could feel the heat radiating off his powerful body. "If you think about it, that's exactly why you're here."

His fingers slid along the crack of my ass before drifting up beneath my hair and gliding across my shoulders. The sensation set me on fire all over again. My pussy clenched, still sensitive from what his teasing tongue had done to it. Despite myself, I moaned at the memory of the fat head of his cock nudging at my entrance before pulling away again.

Don't tease me like this, you asshole . . . you gorgeous fucking asshole!

As if he could feel how desperate I was to come, Ransom smirked, eyeing me like a predator sizing up its prey. His fingers traced circles on my collarbone, around one of my tits, then the nipple, sending tingles down my arms and legs.

"I have so many plans for you, little bunny." His voice dropped to a husky purr. "Plans that will push your limits, make you beg and plead, make you stronger. I intend to thoroughly break you . . . then put you back together again as my perfect little fucktoy."

My heart stuttered at that last word. His intentions should've repulsed me, but instead, I felt another rush of heat between my legs.

For all I knew, 'fucktoy' was his code word for 'warrior destined to kill the Red Queen's Jabberwocky and save Wonderland.' Since there were guests and staff around us, it made sense why he'd talk to me in code.

Ransom leaned down closer to me, brushing his lips over the shell of my ear, whispering so only I could hear him. "You can try to deny it, but I see the truth in your eyes, Alice. You crave submission . . . a firm hand to guide you. To hold you accountable. To teach you discipline."

He gave a gentle tap on the ball gag, making it disappear in another glittering cloud of dust before massaging my jaw. I wiped the drool from my chin onto my shoulder and glared up at him.

"I have *plenty* of discipline!" I hissed under my breath so his bodyguard bunnies couldn't hear. "And why the fuck did you gag me? It's not like I would've told anyone who I was!"

A wicked grin curved his lips as the ball gag reappeared in his hands.

"You can either address me with the respect I deserve, or I

can make it so you don't speak at all. What's it going to be, my pet?"

I squeezed my eyes shut, not wanting to give him the words he demanded.

But he was in a mood.

And I *really* needed to come.

I decided to humor him. At least until I got what I needed.

"I'm sorry . . . my king," I quickly answered, still getting used to not having the ball in my mouth. The gag in Ransom's hand promptly disappeared and was replaced by a gold silk handkerchief.

"There you go. You did well just now," he hummed in approval as he wiped the drool off my face. "To answer your question, I used the gag because my bunnies can be very naughty. I don't trust them alone with you."

"Why not? What would they do to me?"

His eyes lit up while he let out a soft laugh.

"What *wouldn't* they do to you?"

He stroked a finger down my cheek, then my neck, coaxing another traitorous ache of desire from my body.

"Why did you say I have no discipline . . . my king?"

"Because you don't," he replied with a shrug. "Not much, anyway."

I frowned at him.

"I have enough discipline to go to spin class and Pilates three times a week," I informed him. "And I almost never eat junk food."

"You have a personal trainer and a private chef," he pointed out. "If you were truly disciplined, you wouldn't need someone else to make those choices for you. You'd make them on your own."

"I made the decision to hire them," I snapped, quickly adding, "my king."

"You hired them to hold you accountable as a way to avoid holding yourself accountable for your actions."

I faltered for a response. I'd never thought about it that way before.

Had I ever held myself accountable for anything?

When I used to party before an event and puked on the red carpet, I blamed the bartenders for over serving me. When my shoe business imploded for all the world to see, I blamed my venture capitalist boyfriend Remy, but maybe I should've looked into the details first. Maybe I should've done some research before blindly signing papers and throwing money at him.

The longer I thought about it, the more I realized I'd spent more time planning my outfit for the last Met Gala than I did planning my business empire.

Maybe I *wasn't* very disciplined. All I knew was how to outsource my personal responsibilities.

Fucking Ransom.

I hated the idea that he might be right.

"How do you know about my personal trainer and my chef?"

He revealed a sly grin.

"How did the Red Queen know you were here?"

"Dinah . . . I breathed, feeling the pang of betrayal as I said my personal assistant's name out loud. "Chess told me that she works for the queen. Does she work for you, too?"

"Something like that." He gave my leash a little tug. "Come along, my pet. I've bathed you and put a collar on you. Now it's time to feed you."

I followed him over to the table where he prepared a plate for me, filling it with a variety of sliced fruits, veggies, nuts, and lean meat that he carefully cut into small bites. Then he led me over to one of the leather couches.

"Sit."

I sat.

He shook his head. "On the floor."

I wrinkled my nose in disgust. "Excuse me?"

His thumb traced over my lower lip. "My pets aren't allowed to eat on the furniture. You will know your place. Now sit."

Part of me longed to kick him in the face, but I was starving and my pussy still ached. I'd do whatever it took to get my hands free and get myself off.

I sank down to the floor, leaning against the couch, then looked up at him with a flirtatious grin.

"Is this alright, my king?"

He gave a satisfied nod and picked up a small vegetable that looked like a purple carrot. I felt the anticipation rising in my body as he guided the carrot to my lips and slipped it into my mouth. His touch was gentle and intimate, like we were lovers, not captor and captive.

"It's better than alright. It's perfect."

My heart did a backflip at his praise. Damn. Another aching throb pulsed in my clit at the sound of his voice. I stared up at him, torn between my defiance and my desire.

Desire won.

Ransom continued to feed me, offering each bite slowly, never rushing, always savoring the moment, watching intently as I chewed and swallowed. His hands were so gentle as he fed me, offering each morsel to me with a sense of care and tenderness. I almost forgot I was wearing a leash and collar.

With each passing moment I felt my connection to him growing deeper, as if we were sharing a secret language that only we could understand. Every savory bite and sweet crunch in my mouth sent a warmth throughout my body that had nothing to do with the heat of the room.

"Have you had enough, my pet?"

I nodded.

"You can stand up now."

My heart raced as Ransom reached behind me and unfastened my cuffs.

Then my hopes fell as he fastened my wrists together in front of me. I could reach my pussy this way, but I already knew he wouldn't let me.

My mind was racing. How was I going to outwit and over-power the King of Clubs? I was human. He was a demon. He looked a few years older than me, but I didn't know his real age. He probably had centuries of experience in these games of his. I was just a pawn stumbling through his world.

A pawn he *desired*, though.

I knew *all* about desire.

I studied Ransom's reserved, yet insatiable gaze, recognizing the barely contained lust in his eyes as he looked at me. I could use that against him. Seduce him . . . make him believe he had me under his control, and when his guard was down I'd find the Vorpal Sword and run until I found Chess and Hatter.

It was a stupid plan, but it was the only one I could come up with.

I gazed at his handsome face, curious to know how long it would be until he fucked me. My body was my only weapon here, and I needed to use it well. If I was going to play the seduc-tress, I had to act the part. I tossed my long blonde hair and straightened my shoulders, adopting a sultry, playful expression.

"Is there anything I can do for you, my king?"

Just as I'd hoped, his eyes darkened with desire.

"Yes. There is."

My heart fluttered with excitement.

"Obey me, and I will give you everything you need." His hand slid around my tit, stroking and teasing my nipple. Heat flooded my core, and I squeezed my eyes shut.

"Look at me." His voice was sharp. I opened my eyes to find him gazing at me intensely. "You're mine now. Say it."

A violent shiver ran through me at his words, my gaze flick-ering to meet his through my mask. The heat in my belly began to roar, even as I pressed my lips together in a stubborn line.

Ransom's eyes narrowed, and he trailed his fingers down my neck, circling the leather collar.

"Say it," he growled. "Say you belong to me. Say you'll do anything for me."

Ransom's voice was like velvet and dark promises, bringing me right back to the edge where he'd left me. The ache between my legs reignited with a dull throb, then moved to my clit, which was still as swollen and sensitive as it was after he'd licked and sucked me.

His touch burned like fire, searing away my resistance. As the pressure within me built, the words tumbled unbidden from my lips.

"I'm yours, my king," I gasped. "I'll do anything for you. Anything at all."

Ransom nodded in approval, his eyes blazing with triumph. "That's my good little bunny. You deserve a reward for pleasing me."

I watched as he ran one finger down the length of his plate, finally selecting a long-stemmed strawberry, glistening in its own juices. It was such a deep shade of red that it almost looked black. His gaze never left mine as he scooted to the edge of the couch, reached up, and guided the fruit to my lips.

I obediently opened my mouth, but instead of feeding it to me, he ran the tip of it down my chin, my throat, between my breasts, down my belly, and then past my navel.

"You've been so patient. I know how badly you want to come. I can smell how wet you are for me," he said, making me glance away.

"Eyes on me, pet."

I did as I was told.

"You want to get fucked so bad that it hurts, don't you, little bunny?"

I started to bite my lip, then stopped myself.

That was *his* job.

"Yes, my king."

"I can make you come and relieve your pain. Would you like that?"

My eyes lit up with excitement.

"Please, my king!"

"Say it. Tell me exactly what you want."

"Make me come," I shuddered. "Please? I'll do anything for you, my king."

Ransom took the dark strawberry and used his demon magic to elongate it to the shape of a long, fat tongue. Then he traced it along my slit, coating the berry with my juices.

I groaned at the sensation of the cool wetness, of the rough, yet delicious feel of the hard, swollen seeds as they brushed against my clit.

"How does that feel?" he murmured as he rubbed the fruit up and down my slit. "Tell me."

"It feels amazing," I whimpered. He shook his head.

"You can do better than that. Rest your arms on my shoulders, and tell me exactly what these sensations feel like."

I did as he instructed, learning forward and draping my arms around his neck, then rested on his strong shoulders. It was so intimate, almost hugging him while he played with my pussy.

"It's cool and wet," I sighed in his ear. "And the seeds are kinda ticklish, but the texture feels so good." I pressed my hips forward, hoping to get more friction.

"What about this?" He spread my lips with one hand, making circles around my clit with the strawberry. The hard seeds on the top of the fruit made me writhe in his grasp. "How does this feel?"

"Rough, but I like it," I moaned. "I don't want it to stop."

"I have to stop, otherwise I can't do this."

Two fingers coated themselves in my juice before sinking into my pussy, and I groaned in relief as they began to stretch and explore my aching core.

63

"Remember that you're mine," he whispered, still pumping his fingers inside me, still massaging my clit with the strawberry. "Your pleasure belongs to me. I decide *when* my bunny gets to fuck . . . and *how* she gets fucked. Do you understand?"

"Yes, my king," I shuddered in between breaths.

"Repeat it back to me so I know you understand."

"You decide when I get to fuck, and *how* I get fucked."

"Yes I do," he hummed in satisfaction. "Sit on my lap and watch me fuck you."

He withdrew his hard, warm fingers to let me straddle his legs. I kept glancing at his crotch, wondering when he was going to take out his cock.

"Eyes on me, bunny. Don't forget that I decide *how* you get fucked."

"I'm sorry, my king," I apologized. Then something long and fat and cool and textured burrowed deep into my pussy. I let out a gasp at the strange sensation, squirming and arching my back in response.

Is he actually fucking me with a giant strawberry?

Yes, he was.

He must've been, because there wasn't a dick in the world that felt like what I was experiencing. I rode harder against his hand, meeting every thrust. In that moment, I didn't care what he fucked me with—I just wanted to come.

"Stop trying to fuck and hold still," he warned. "*I'm* the one fucking *you*. I'll let you watch as long as you hold still."

Panting now, I nodded and bowed my head, watching in disbelief as he grasped the long stem and plunged the dark fruit deeper and deeper into me.

"Look at the wanton slut you are, so desperate for my cock that you're willing to let me fuck you with a piece of fruit," he said in my ear, his cheek hot, his breath warm on my skin. "Are you my slutty little bunny?"

"Oh, fuck yeah I am," I hissed through my teeth. I swallowed hard, hating how much I craved his touch . . . even if he was using a giant piece of fruit. It was all I could do not to thrust my hips against him.

"Your pleasure belongs to me. You don't come unless I allow it," he said, lifting a stern brow. I immediately nodded in compliance. "When I tell you to come, I want you to look at me and come."

"Yes, my king," I sighed, clenching my inner walls on the fruit.

He pulled it out and rubbed it against my clit, the hard little seeds itching a scratch I'd had for *way* too long. The berry was warm now, heated up from the fire burning in my core. The skin of the fruit slipped and glided against my clit, then dove back into my channel before pulling out and massaging me some more.

"Ransom—" I panted, and the severe look he gave me reminded me I'd just broken one of his rules.

Don't say his name. *Ever.*

"I'm sorry! I mean, my king! Oh, fuck!"

"Come for me, little bunny," he urged, his eyes hungry, his voice brimming with pure lust. "Show me what I've done to you."

I stared straight into his gorgeous face as I crested over the edge. He rubbed the rough seeds of the berry against my swollen clit one more time, then plunged it into me with a smooth thrust, stretching my tight heat as I convulsed all around it.

Wave after wave of pleasure crashed through me, wringing every ounce of euphoria from my body, soaking my thighs in hot sweat. I didn't even realize how loud I was moaning in his ear until it was joined by Ransom's wicked laugh.

With my shackled arms still draped around his shoulders, I looked at him in a daze, feeling completely drained and utterly satisfied. Aftershocks rippled through me at will, jerking my body against his.

"Oh, Alice . . . you were magnificent," he groaned in my ear as he held me close. "Absolutely incredible." His hands caressed my hair, my arms, and my back as I caught my breath.

Pride surged within me. Pride in knowing that I'd impressed someone who was no doubt *very* hard to please.

I didn't know if it was the high from the long-awaited full-body orgasm or something else, but when Ransom said those words to me, I clung to them. I clung to *him*.

I'd made him proud.

He'd made me feel something I'd never felt before, which was saying a lot since fucking was one of the only things I was good at, and I'd recently started fucking guys two at a time.

As I came out of the orgasmic fog, I noticed I was sweating, but Ransom's jacket, his shirt, and his lap were drenched.

"Why's everything so wet?" I asked. "Did the strawberry explode?"

"No," he answered with a seductive smile. He ran his hand along one of my arms that rested on his shoulder. "*You* did. All over me."

Speechless, I watched as he pulled the strawberry out of my pussy and took a generous bite of it. Then another.

I watched in bewilderment until I realized what he was saying—I'd squirted all over him.

"Ransom—I mean—my king—I'm, I'm *so* sorry!" I stammered as my face went red. Humiliated, I tried to pull away, but he held me in place. "I've never done anything like this before!"

"Then I'll have to make you do it again," he chuckled before taking another bite of the strawberry.

"But . . . your clothes," I babbled, half convinced I might die of sheer embarrassment. "Holy shit . . . I ruined your suit!"

"It's fine," he replied with a nonchalant shrug, and set the stem of the strawberry back on the plate. "Did you enjoy what I did to you?"

Realizing he wasn't upset in the slightest, I nodded my head.

"Do you want me to make you come again?"

My eyes lit up and my pussy clenched with excitement. Did he even have to ask? I wanted his hot mouth on me, licking and sucking, fingers fucking. I licked my lips, hoping he was going to strip off his wet clothes and take me for a spin on that monster cock of his.

"Absolutely, my king," I grinned.

"Do you want me to fuck you?" he growled in my ear. "Does my slutty little bunny want to hippity-hop on my cock and bounce, bounce, bounce until she comes, comes comes?"

"Oh . . . *please*, my king," I whimpered.

"Then you'll have to earn it," he said coolly.

He peeled me off of him and rose to his feet, then snapped his fingers. In an instant, he was wearing a different black suit, this one covered in tiny gold embroidered clubs.

He tugged on my leash and led me to the partition overlooking his domain, then clapped his hands. Within seconds, all of the music and chatter in the club quieted as everyone's eyes turned to him.

"Attention, everyone! Tonight we have a special treat for you at The Rabbit Hole," he announced, raising his voice to address the crowd. "I've just acquired a new bunny."

A ripple of interest went around the room at his news, and I felt myself shrink away from their prying eyes. Ransom grasped my leash and dragged me back to his side, putting me on display. He shot me a wicked grin, then motioned for his revelers to be quiet.

"Yes, yes, you know what that means—one of them has to go! So place your bets, ladies and gentlemen! The Bunny Bondage Games are about to begin!"

CHAPTER
FIVE
ALICE

The Bunny Bondage Games?

What the actual *fuck* had I just gotten myself into?

The crowd roared as Ransom tugged on my leather collar and escorted me into the heart of the casino floor. The Tweedles followed close behind.

I wasn't getting out of this . . . whatever it was.

Games of pleasure and games of chance came to a halt as Ransom cut a path through the crowd. Even the exotic dancers stopped twirling on their poles to watch, their attentive eyes glittering behind their bunny masks. The scent of sweat and sex and excitement permeated the air, forming tendrils of arousal that coiled low in my belly.

Ransom's lips curled into a sly smirk, his eyes gleaming with wicked promises as he leaned down to speak to me.

"Welcome to my playground, little bunny. Are you ready to play a game?"

The residual scent of strawberries and my pussy lingered on his breath, reminding me of the twisted pleasure I'd just experienced at his hands. Heat flooded my cheeks at the memory of coming for him, coming in his lap. I wanted to hate him, but his magnetism was a drug.

If I wasn't careful, he'd become an addiction.

He'd consume my every waking thought.

I had to fight it while I still could.

I straightened, tilting my chin up in cocky defiance.

"Not really . . . my king. I'm ready for Netflix and a glass of wine."

I was nowhere near ready for whatever depraved games this incubus had in store. I still didn't know what an incubus demon was, but I was leaning strongly toward 'infuriating and twisted sex freak.'

"Such fire," he chuckled, clearly amused by my attitude. "Let's see if it serves you well in the competition."

My heart pounded against my ribcage as the guests swarmed around us, evaluating me in hushed, excited tones.

"Strong legs . . . this new girl seems built to run and climb," one of them said, eyeing my lower body.

"Or hold on tight for the ride of her life!" another guest laughed, and started counting out gold chips.

They were placing bets on us contestants—Ransom's sex bunnies. A shiver ran down my spine as I realized I was now one of them.

We stopped in front of a giant boxing ring that could've held at least thirty people. Maybe fifty. The same gold bunny emblem from the club's doors was printed on the center of the black mat, with gold posts and ropes to keep the contestants inside.

I swallowed hard, acutely aware of the weight of the bunny ears and the mask hiding my face from everyone. My only comfort was the fact that I was completely anonymous.

"Alright, ladies and gentlemen . . . and bunnies," Ransom announced, his voice dripping with sinister charm as it filled the room. "Tonight's first challenge of the Bunny Bondage Games is . . . a pillow fight!"

Cheers and cries of excitement filled the space around me, and more money and chips changed hands.

A pillow fight? I couldn't help but scoff at the idea. How could something so stupid and childish be part of this twisted competition?

"Seriously?" I said, rolling my eyes at Ransom. "A pillow fight? What's next, a game of musical chairs?"

Ransom's dark eyes lit up with so many flecks of gold that they appeared to glow. The diabolical grin on his face made me wish I'd kept my mouth shut.

"That's an *outstanding* suggestion, my pet. I'll make sure we play that tomorrow night," he replied. His gaze never left mine as he unlocked my wrists and handed my leash to one of the Tweedles. "Underestimate these games at your own peril, little bunny. You'll soon learn that even the most banal tasks can test your limits in ways you never imagined."

I continued to eye him skeptically as he climbed into the center of the ring, faced the crowd, and explained the rules.

"Every bunny is allowed one pillow, no more, no less. If a bunny is disarmed or drops their pillow, they're disqualified. If the round ends and a bunny keeps fighting, they're disqualified. If a bunny falls out of the ring or leaves the ring for *any* reason, they're disqualified."

"What if they're thrown out of the ring?" a guest called out from the crowd.

"Disqualified!"

Ransom's answer was met with more chatter and bets from his guests.

"The pillow fight will have three rounds. Guests of The Rabbit Hole will vote on the bunnies left standing at the end of the final round. First place in tonight's pillow fight gets an advantage in the next event of the Bunny Bondage Games."

He waved over a huge referee wearing a gold whistle, a black helmet, and black body armor. It wasn't the lightweight equestrian vest and helmet like my older sister Marcella used when she rode her horses. It was the kind of protection that one of my college boyfriends wore when he was racing his Ducati.

Something wasn't adding up.

If this was just a pillow fight, why was the ref prepared for a motorcycle accident?

He blew the whistle to get everyone's attention.

"Round one begins in five minutes!"

A giant digital clock appeared on the wall behind the ring, plastering a countdown until the start of the first round.

I started to formulate a strategy in my head, which mostly consisted of not dropping my pillow and not getting thrown out of the ring. But as I glanced around at the other bunnies, they didn't look like a bunch of teenagers at a co-ed slumber party. Their eyes were filled with determination and hunger for victory.

Trippy and Caramel were busy whispering with the other bunnies, their icy glares making it clear that they saw me as a threat. I knew I was an outsider, but this was ridiculous. We were all adults here, but those bitches were acting like middle school mean girls.

Pillows of all shapes and sizes began appearing in the other bunnies' hands, making me nervous. The bigger pillows were going to send me flying. The smaller ones would probably hurt more.

I thought of the pillows on my bed back home in Malibu . . . they were stuffed with Canadian goose down, covered in hot pink faux fur on one side, and pink and purple sequins on the other. I stared at my empty hands, willing a pillow into them with all my imagination.

Nothing happened.

"Listen up, my pet," Ransom said, suddenly at my side. He unfastened my leash and knelt down in front of me, lowering his voice so that only I could hear him. "I've just given you the perfect opportunity to accelerate your training. You have the potential to excel in this competition, but you'll have to be more resourceful, more resilient, and more strategic than any of these bunnies. You'll need to push yourself beyond your comfort zone to reach that potential. It won't be easy for you."

"Thanks for the vote of confidence, my king," I muttered, feeling nervous at how many bunnies were climbing into the ring. There were definitely more than thirty. I looked up at Ransom, putting my hands on my naked hips.

"Hey, how come I can't imagine anything into being real? When I was with Chess and Hatter I could imagine a dress and then I was wearing it. Why isn't that working here?"

"You don't have that power while you're in my custody," Ransom said, glancing at my collar before quickly settling his eyes back onto mine. "What kind of pillow would you like to fight with?"

The moment I described the one back home on my bed, it was in his hands. Surrounded by black and gold elegance, he looked ridiculous holding such a foo-foo hot pink pillow. He offered it to me, then hesitated, giving me a cautious look.

"Do you want it just like this, as it is? Or do you want it enhanced for the fight?"

"What do you mean, *enhanced*?" I asked, looking around at the other bunnies. Their pillows were different shapes and sizes and colors, but they were still just pillows. "You mean with ruffles or something?"

Ransom slowly shook his head.

"No, I don't mean with ruffles," he deadpanned. "I mean with *something*."

"Something like what?" I hissed in frustration as I glanced at the countdown clock on the wall. The first round was about to start. "You mean like have it filled with rocks instead of feathers?"

"Filling it with rocks would make it too heavy for you to lift," he said, rising to his feet. The timer had less than ten seconds left.

"You'd better hop along, bunny. If you're not in the ring when the whistle blows, you'll be disqualified."

Clutching my fluffy pink pillow against my naked chest, I ran towards the ring and climbed in just as the referee blew the whistle.

The moment the first round began, chaos erupted throughout the entire casino.

The fight seemed innocent enough at first—just a group of naked men and women in bunny masks engaged in a playful battle with soft, fluffy pillows.

The innocence didn't last long.

I ducked and dodged pillows, trying my best to avoid the fray. I was hit in the back of my knees and flung to the ground by a strike meant for someone else.

From the safety of the floor, I watched in disbelief as Ransom's favorite bunny with the black curls picked up a petite brunette half his size. Holding his pillow in one hand, he tossed her through the gold ropes and out of the ring with the other. Instead of helping her up, the guests standing around her started making new bets.

I scrambled to my feet, clinging to my pillow for dear life, using it as a shield until I found a space to regroup. Within seconds, I was cornered by Trippy, Caramel, and a few of their friends, all ganging up on me with ruthless determination. No matter how hard I tried, I couldn't seem to land a single solid hit on any of them.

Trippy yelled at her friends to back up away from me, and for a split second I wondered if I'd misjudged her. She drew back her arm, and a sudden, searing pain exploded in my head as her pillow made contact. It felt like a thousand white-hot needles piercing my skull all at once.

My vision blurred, and the room began to tilt, then spin uncontrollably. The last thing I heard before darkness swallowed me was the sound of the referee's whistle as my body hit the mat.

I came to with a gasp, blinking up at the chandeliers overhead. A dull ache throbbed at the back of my skull, although the blinding pain from before had dulled to a manageable level.

"That's the end of Round one! Five minutes until the next round!" the referee bellowed. Meanwhile, I lay there, struggling to make sense of what had just happened.

By some kind of miracle, I was still clinging onto my pillow.

I could feel Ransom's presence before I saw him. His intoxicating scent filled my nostrils, drowning out the pain. As my eyes fluttered in confusion, I found myself gazing into his concerned face.

"Are you alright, Alice?" he whispered, his voice laced with genuine worry. I let him help me sit up but immediately regretted it as nausea washed over me. I'd already ruined one of his suits this evening. I didn't want to puke on him and ruin another.

"No, I'm not alright," I groaned, clutching my throbbing head. "I can't do this for two more rounds. Let me get out of the ring. Please?"

"Listen to me," Ransom said, gripping my shoulders. "You're stronger than you think. You just need to change your strategy. Don't play harder. Play smarter."

"I think that blue-haired bitch has a brick in her pillowcase," I told him as I rubbed my head. "That's why it hurts so much."

"Probably," Ransom agreed with a nod. His lips curled into a sinister smile as he patted my pillow. "Which is precisely why I've just put razor wire in yours."

My eyes widened in shock. I glanced down at my hot pink pillow covered in faux fur and sequins. Was it really full of razor wire? I dunked it on the mat a couple of times, hearing the distinct sound of coiled metal inside.

"What the *fuck*?" I squeaked. "Is this even allowed?"

He raised a sly eyebrow at me.

"You heard the rules. I never said it *wasn't* allowed."

My heart raced, torn between gratitude for Ransom's help and horror at the idea of using such a brutal weapon.

"It just doesn't seem fair," I told him as I rubbed my aching head. I gazed past his shoulders at the other bunnies milling around the ring. At least half of them had been disqualified in the first round, and were now licking their wounds from the other side of the gold ropes.

"Do you want to play fair, or do you want to play to *win?*" Ransom caressed my cheek, trailing his fingers down to grasp my chin. He pinned his calculating eyes on me, waiting for an answer.

"I wanna win," I said softly.

Ransom's eyes narrowed at me, growing more intense by the millisecond.

"Then act like it," he growled. He let go of my chin and crawled outside the ropes, dropping gracefully to the floor outside the ring. And all the while, his intense stare never left my face.

The ref's whistle blew again. As round two got underway, I quickly realized that this was never meant to be an ordinary slumber party game. The other bunnies were ruthless, their pillows transforming into deadly weapons as they swung them with brutal force against each other.

"Damn it!" I cursed as a small pillow struck me in the stomach, knocking the wind out of me. I doubled over, unsure if the pillow was full of marbles or metal washers.

Then she hit me again.

Marbles. Those were definitely marbles.

I looked up just in time to see Caramel preparing for another swing at me while Trippy and her squad started heading towards me. I shrieked, scrambling to defend myself, panic and adrenaline shooting through my bloodstream.

Blows rained down on me from all sides, the bunnies working together with ruthless efficiency.

Fuck, fuck, fuck!

I was outnumbered and overpowered, no match for their combined strength. Pain exploded across my body as fists, marbles, and Trippy's brick struck me.

I struggled to fend them off. I was up, dodging and weaving as best I could while managing to land a few mediocre blows of my own.

The whistle blew, cutting through the chaos like a knife through warm butter. The bunnies retreated instantly, fading back against the gold ropes of the ring.

I scanned the room, searching for Ransom. I jumped when I realized he was standing at the edge of the mat. He was watching me, arms crossed over his chest.

He looked pissed.

"What the fuck are you doing in there?" he demanded through clenched teeth.

"Trying not to get the shit kicked out of me!" I snapped back. His eyes flashed at my insolence, but I didn't care. If he wanted me to be obedient, then he should've kept me on my leash and out of this fight.

He motioned for me to kneel down to him. He wasn't going to crawl in the ring and coddle me this time.

"Callister told me that you knew how to attack and defend, so why aren't you doing it?"

"Uh, maybe because I studied fencing, not this insane bull-shit!" I argued, shaking the fuzzy hot pink pillow in his face. The coils of razor wire inside rattled gently among the feathers. "What if I accidentally kill someone?"

"This is a controlled environment. They'll be fine," Ransom said through tight lips. "The magic of imagination heals all things in Wonderland."

"Then why isn't mine working?" I demanded, pointing at the

leather collar around my neck. "Why did you take my power away? You're making me fight at a disadvantage!"

"A disadvantage?" he scoffed. "You're the only bunny I'm instructing tonight. Regarding your imagination, you haven't proven yourself responsible enough to be given that privilege. You have to earn it, just like all the other bunnies," he said, still frowning at me.

"Ugh! How long is that gonna take?"

Clearly doing his best to temper his anger in front of his guests, Ransom clenched his jaw and shot me a cold smile that didn't reach his eyes.

"That depends entirely on you. I'm doing all of this for your benefit, and you're being nothing but unappreciative." He leaned closer and reached through the ropes, hooking his finger on the gold ring of my collar. Then he pulled me close. "Callister and I have a wager on whether you'll succeed or not," he snarled, his tone severe. "If you're so selfish that you aren't willing to fight for Wonderland, stop wasting my time and get out of the ring."

He had a bet with Callister about me? What the fuck? It was obvious which one of them had bet against me. For all I knew, Callister was in the crowd, watching me, placing more bets on me, expecting me to fail.

Anger roiled up inside me as I thought of that slimy caterpillar. I'd called him a worm the last time I saw him, but he wasn't even that. He was scheming, two-faced snake.

Ransom started to pull me towards him. I dug my heels into the mat and held my ground, refusing to crawl through the gold ropes.

"Oh, so now you want to stay and play?" he mocked, still holding onto my collar.

"I'm not here to play," I snapped, tightening my grasp on my pillow. "I'm here to win!"

"Then prove it," said Ransom as he let go of me and took a step back. All the coldness left him as his gaze took on a heated, hungry look. It was the kind of look that said he couldn't wait to fuck me when this was all over. "Do keep in mind that you're swimming with sharks now, bunny."

He paused to give me a seductive wink.

"So be a fucking shark."

The whistle rang through the room and I sprang into action. Gritting my teeth, I channeled my years of experience in competitive fencing. Hopefully all that time in private school was about to pay off.

I focused on my opponents' movements, anticipating their attacks and countering them with precision. Every swing of my pillow sent a few feathers and sequins flying through the air. It wasn't long before I started to find my rhythm, and as the round wore on, I began to feel a strange sense of exhilaration.

My gaze landed on Trippy, who was glaring at me with unveiled hatred.

Good. Let her hate me.

It would make defeating her all the sweeter.

She shared a look with Caramel and their friends, then came for me. I couldn't let myself be defeated so easily—not by Trippy and Caramel, and definitely not in front of Ransom.

With a vicious roar, I hurled my pillow at her naked body as hard as I could, catching her off guard and sending her sprawling to the ground. The entire left side of her body was cut to ribbons.

I ran after one of the door bunnies next, slicing across his ass, giving him a few extra cracks. More blood-stained feathers and sequins fluttered around me. I was about to go after Caramel when I heard the kind of scream that chilled me to the bone.

I whipped around to see Ransom's favorite bunny, the black haired one, beating the shit out Trippy from where she lay on the mat. Although she was down, she was refusing to let go of her pillow, meaning she was still a contender. This guy twice her size was smacking his huge pillow against the wounds I'd given her.

Every blow sent more of her blood spraying in every direction, making her scream in agony.

I caught a glimpse of her stark white ribs poking through the mangled flesh. When I realized that this dickhead wasn't going to quit hurting her until she gave up, something inside of me snapped.

All I could see was hot pink faux fur, white down feathers dripping in blood, and sequins . . . so many sequins, as I attacked the man brutalizing Trippy. My razor wire pillow tore his arm and his back to shreds and left him dripping in red. There was so much blood that when the hulking asshole whirled around to fight me, he slipped and fell in the puddle of his own making.

Hot pink and purple sequins stuck to his bloody skin as I raged on him. Every time his body writhed, it glittered and sparkled under the lights. Eventually Caramel joined in and helped me drag his pillow out of his hands.

"Disqualified!" the ref yelled.

Caramel and I jumped up and down, shrieking and laughing at our victory.

Our moment didn't last very long.

I think she and I both realized that we'd have to fight each other next. She took a step away from me, glancing at the pool of blood that Trippy and Dickface—because that was his name now —were lying in.

I wiped the sweat out of my eyes and looked around the ring. There were only a handful of us bunnies left. Trippy, Caramel, the two guys from the front doors, and a couple others. I glanced at the clock. Four seconds remained.

"Hey fuckers," I called to the door bunnies. "Afraid to fight me?"

Two more seconds.

With surly frowns, they both came running at me.

I ducked and covered myself just as the ref's whistle blew for the last time. I braced myself for their impacts, taking them with a groan. Although it hurt, I stopped thinking about the pain the moment the referee pointed at them and shouted, "Disqualified!"

I sat up and watched them both try to argue, but they'd broken the rules—they'd hit me after the whistle blew and everyone saw it.

"You stupid blonde bitch!" one of them snarled at me.

"You'll pay for that!" growled the other.

I just smiled and waved my middle finger at them.

"You're not stupid," said a soft, yet strong voice beside me. "*They* are."

I turned to see Caramel standing by my side.

"Those dipshits did it to themselves," I panted with a faint smile, trying to catch my breath. "Thanks for not attacking me when you had the chance."

Her warm brown eyes flicked down to my pillowcase, which was in tatters. Silver razor wire dripping with blood poked out of the shredded pink fur.

"Likewise. I know the injuries don't last, but still . . . I'd rather avoid it."

She glanced over her shoulder, eyeing her friend. I followed her over to check on Trippy, who was already having her injury healed by a member of the Rabbit Hole staff. Sure enough, the gaping wound in her side was gone. Her skin was being patched up by gentle currents of barely visible energy.

"Are you okay?"

Trippy glowered up at me.

"Go suck on a hookah, new bitch!"

"Awesome," I replied without missing a beat. "Fuck you, too!"

I turned on my heel and wandered to the edge of the ring where Ransom was already waiting for me. My heart did a backflip when I caught his proud smile.

"Look at you, making friends already," he teased.

"Not her," I said, thumbing over my shoulder at Trippy. "Talk about an ungrateful cow."

"She's angry that you made her look weak," he shrugged as he climbed into the ring with me and the last remaining bunnies. "Let's see what the audience thought of your performance."

He motioned to three platforms that were positioned in the center of the ring where Trippy and Dickface's blood had been. Then he joined the referee as the guests of the Rabbit Hole voted on the best fighter.

First place went to one of the biggest boy bunnies, who'd taken out almost a quarter of the competition on his own. Second place went to Trippy, for her leadership skills, which I thought was a crock of shit.

I held my breath as third place was announced, and was shocked to hear it go to Caramel for her ability to work with others.

I bit down on my lip, clapping weakly with everyone else.

It should've gone to *me*!

I'm the one who saved Trippy from Dickface. I should've gotten a podium! But no . . . I was the new girl. The awards all went to familiar faces.

"Congratulations," Ransom said to me, draping a thick black sash across my shoulder.

"For what?" I asked above the cheers and clapping.

"The audience just awarded you Bunny of the Day." He adjusted my sash, then lifted my arm to make me wave at the crowd gathered around the ring. I felt his breath fall against my neck as he lowered his head to whisper in my ear.

"And I've just awarded you Bunny of the Evening."

CHAPTER
SIX
RANSOM

I reveled in Alice's mix of anticipation, excitement, and trepidation as I clipped on her leash and fastened her wrist cuffs back together. Although I hadn't expected her to take a podium, I was thrilled that she'd won "Bunny of the Day" in the Bunny Bondage Games.

I hadn't made it easy for her, but the sinners of Wonderland had spoken.

They were just as dazzled by her fire as I was.

True, I had to push her in the right direction, but that's what training was all about. She fought so viciously to win, yet it completely surprised me that she could still be merciful.

Now it was time for her *real* reward.

Me.

I led her through the maze of black hallways, designed to look exactly the same so she wouldn't be able to escape without help. I pushed open the door to my bedroom . . . my sanctuary, and brought her into the heart of my kingdom.

This was where I truly came alive.

I prided myself on keeping the furnishings simple, tasteful, yet seductive. The beauty of Wonderland was that imagination had the power to rule over nearly everything . . . aside from the Red Queen.

Imagination let me pick and choose what bondage equipment to display, and what to hide until it was desired.

Wanted.

Necessary.

Nothing took me out of a scene faster than filth, cheapness, or too much of the wrong thing at the wrong time.

Gold framed mirrors reflected the warm flickering candle-light as Alice and I stopped near a small tub in the center of the black and gold tiled floor. My pet was in need of another bath. Her wounds from the pillow fight had been healed in the ring, but there was still dried blood and sweat and glittering sequins sticking to her skin.

I snickered at the thought.

She'd be wearing thick strings of pearls when I was done with her.

"Alice, are you going to be a good girl for me and wash your-self?" I asked.

Her eyes darted around the room, drinking in every sinful detail, watching her reflection in one of the many mirrors. I could almost see the wheels turning in her head, trying to imagine what lay in store for her.

She had no fucking idea . . . and I loved it.

"Y—yes, my king," she stammered, her voice barely above a whisper. My cock twitched at hearing her address me properly. She was learning so fast.

"That's what I wanted to hear," I said with an approving nod. "The sooner you get clean, the sooner I get to play with my little fuck toy."

I removed her bunny mask, revealing her flushed cheeks and wild eyes. She wanted to get fucked so bad that I could already smell her cunt getting slick for me.

Luckily there'd be more where that came from.

She stepped gingerly into the tub and began to sponge off her arms and legs, ensuring every inch of her skin was clean. She quickly washed her hair, then dipped under the water to rinse the bubbles from her long, golden mane. I imagined grabbing two fistfuls of it and riding her into my mattress, hanging on as she kicked and bucked against me.

Soon.

But not tonight.

I had to resist the urge. We still had much work to do.

My cock hardened as she put on a flirtatious little show of spreading her legs, bending over, and washing the deep groove in her peach of an ass.

"My slutty little bunny is making me so proud this evening," I told her. "Let's see how long you keep it up."

I snapped my fingers, making the tub disappear. I quickly dried Alice off, then blindfolded her and restrained her hands behind her back, leaving her vulnerable and at my mercy.

"Ransom, w—what's happening?" she asked, her voice trembling as I guided her feet to step into a special leather harness.

"Shhh." I pressed a finger to her lips, then continued sliding the harness up her legs, buckling it around her slender waist. "You'll find out soon enough."

I could sense her confusion, her fear, her curiosity, and her lust all mingling together, creating a heady cocktail that intoxicated me as much as it did her.

When I lifted her into my arms, her legs wrapped around my waist, pressing her wet gash against my belly, her warmth taunting me to throw her down and sink into her heat.

Damn.

This was going to be harder than I thought.

No wonder Chess had stuffed his massive cock into her the first chance he got.

No wonder Hatter had ridden her ass into such oblivion that

she stayed asleep when the Tweedles had found her and brought her to me.

Now it was *my* turn.

I laid Alice down on the soft black silk sheets, my eyes lingering on her glistening slit for a moment before I proceeded to tie her arms and legs to the corners of my bed. Her thighs trembled beneath my touch, and I could feel the heat emanating from her core.

With each passing second, her clit started to swell, throbbing with need, her slick folds parting like the petals of a blossoming flower.

"Ransom," she breathed, her voice strained and desperate. "Please . . ."

"Patience, my pet," I replied, my voice calm yet dripping with dark intent. I crawled onto the bed, positioning myself between her spread legs, and lowered my head towards her exposed pussy.

I studied it carefully, taking note of the particular shade of pink, of how plump the shiny lips had become. The scent of her arousal stirred something primal within me—a hunger that demanded satisfaction.

I started teasing her with my mouth, nipping at her swollen lips, lapping her hard little clit and drinking her wetness. My fingers joined in soon after, sliding inside her tight entrance and curling just right to elicit a moan of pleasure from her lips.

"Oh, fuck," she gasped, her hips riding steadily against my hand, seeking more of the delicious friction I provided.

"You like getting fucked by me, don't you?" I murmured.

"Yeah," she whimpered. "Please, my king . . . please fuck me."

I reached for an array of toys laid out in front of me. Each one was designed to provide a unique sensation that would push Alice further into the realm of ecstasy . . . the realm where I excelled.

A smooth glass dildo, cold to the touch, sent her spine into an arch as I slid it slowly inside her. The way her pussy clenched around it made my cock ache with envy.

Next, I toyed with a deeply ribbed silicone vibrator, the ridges providing extra stimulation as it filled her completely. Her moans grew louder, more desperate as I continued to tease her and fuck her with a variety of textures and sensations:

Hard . . .

Thick . . .

Soft . . .

Curved . . .

Every reaction she gave, every quiver and cry, fed my own desires, my incubus appetite, driving me to push her further.

I wanted to see all of her holes stuffed at the same time.

"My king, please . . . I need more . . . " Alice's voice cracked, her body writhing in an exquisite mix of pleasure and frustration.

"Tell me what you need," I demanded, my fingers working expertly to bring her closer and closer to the edge without letting her tumble over.

"Please, just . . . just fuck me already!" she whimpered, her voice full of longing.

"Patience, bunny," I reminded her, my voice both gentle and firm. "You'll get what you need when I say so. Do you understand?"

"Yeah."

"Who decides when you get to fuck?"

"You do."

More blood coursed through my cock, making it swell so hard that I had no choice but to stop and strip out of my clothes.

"Are you ready for more?" I asked, my voice low and seductive. She nodded, her chest heaving with each breath as she anticipated what would come next.

"Then let's explore a different part of you," I said, crawling back onto the bed. I conjured a large pillow shaped like a wedge, then slid it under my pet until my face was level with her ass. Her mouth sucked in a gasp of surprise, but she didn't protest.

I lowered my mouth to her tightest hole, wetting it with my tongue before beginning a slow, sensual assault. Her body tensed at first, unused to the sensation, but as I continued to lick and tease, she relaxed and began to moan in pleasure.

"Ransom, what are you—oh fuck!" she gasped as I pressed the rounded tip of a slick metal plug against her orifice. I watched with satisfaction as the flare of the plug stretched her tight hole, little by little, until it was swallowed by her greedy flesh.

Despite the blindfold, the look on her face was one of shock, fear, and a hint of newfound desire. It fueled me further, knowing that I was pushing her boundaries and helping her discover parts of herself she never knew existed.

"Trust me, Alice," I murmured, my fingers brushing against her swollen clit as I slowly pulled the toy out of her and pushed it deeper inside. "You'll learn to love this."

"I already love it, my king," she admitted, her voice a mix of apprehension and arousal. Her raw honesty and vulnerability were intoxicating. It only made me want her more.

"Let's see how much more you can take," I challenged, reaching for a set of gold nipple clamps connected by a delicate chain. Alice's mouth twisted into a grimace as I fastened the clamps around her sensitive nipples, causing her to gasp in pain and pleasure.

Then I slipped the butt plug out of her ass, replacing it with one substantially bigger.

"Who decides *how* you fuck?" I asked, my voice dark and teasing.

"You do," she groaned, her breaths coming in short gasps as the clamps tightened even harder around her nipples.

"Good girl. I love watching how well you play with my toys."

As I continued to torment Alice with a mix of pleasure and pain, spreading her hole around the smooth metal plug, I could see her emotions shifting. I knew she was moving away from the spoiled little brat and closer to becoming a fierce, obedient warrior. With each new sensation, I watched her learn more about her body, her desires, and her limits.

"It's too much," she moaned, her voice pleading. "I . . . I don't think I can take much more."

"I think you can," I replied, a wicked smile playing across my lips. "I need to know what my slutty little bunny can handle."

Leaning down, my lips found her swollen clit once more, and I let my tongue swirl over its sensitive surface as I pumped the plug in and out of her ass. She moaned and writhed beneath me, the pleasure building within her.

"Please, my king," she whimpered, thrashing in her restraints, "it's too much . . . I can't . . . "

"Shhh," I whispered against her slick flesh. "Trust me, Alice. I know *exactly* what you need."

I sucked on her clit, feeling her body tense as she approached the edge of orgasm. Just before she could fall into the abyss of ecstasy, I pulled away, denying her the release she craved. The frustration in her breathy moans only fueled my desire to continue our torturous game.

"Please . . . " she begged, her voice barely audible.

"Patience, my pet," I reminded her, a wicked smile tugging at my lips. "You've come so far already. Let's see how much further I can take you."

I moved to the assortment of toys I had prepared earlier, selecting two different sizes of one of my favorites: whimsy whirls.

Attaching one to the harness around her waist and thighs, I slowly pushed it deep into her dark channel. Alice gasped, her restrained legs twisting her hips against the wedge cushion under her ass.

I watched in pleasure as the whimsy whirl stretched her tight opening and began to move inside of her.

"What the fuck is that?" she cried out, her body tensing against the intrusion.

"It's called a whimsy whirl," I murmured, my fingers tracing soothing circles on her trembling thighs.

"What the hell is a whimsy whirl?" she blurted out, gritting her teeth as it sped up.

"It's a toy I designed for filling holes," I explained with a grin. I lifted the larger one, inspecting it carefully. It was essentially an artificial muscle covered in a smooth purple skin. I created it to wiggle and thicken on demand, at various levels of intensity, thanks to a dial on the outside.

"I'm somewhat of an inventor. When you're an immortal demon, you have a lot of time on your hands."

I reached down and turned the dial up one more level.

"How's it moving like that?" she gasped. "Is it alive?"

"Not in the slightest," I assured her. "But it certainly feels like it, doesn't it?"

"Yeah . . . oh fuck! I've never felt anything like it!"

"You can handle it, Alice. I know you can. Now be a good little fuck toy and take another one for me."

Before she could argue, I took the other whimsy whirl and connected it to the same harness, above the first one. With a teasing brush against her wet pussy, I slid it inside, filling her completely. The toys moved within her, their prehensile nature allowing them to twist and thrust as if they had minds of their own.

The wails of shock and pleasure filled my room, bouncing off the mirrors.

"Holy fuck . . . What are you doing to me?" Alice panted. Her whole body writhed under my power as she struggled to process the overwhelming sensations coursing through her.

"I'm showing you what you're capable of." My fingers danced over her nipple clamps before adjusting the intensity of the whimsy whirls' movements. "You're being such a good little slut for me. Embrace it. This is only the beginning."

As the toys continued their relentless dance within her, I could see Alice's resolve begin to crumble. She was no longer simply submitting to the experience; she was becoming an active participant in her own pleasure.

"My king," she whispered, her voice trembling with need. "I want . . . I need . . . please . . . "

"Tell me, Alice," I urged, my voice low and seductive. "What does my little fuck toy need?"

"More," she breathed, her nails digging into her palms as the toys pushed her closer and closer to the edge. "Please, give me more."

"Would you like to watch yourself get fucked?"

"Yes!" she half cried, half roared.

I stretched out beside her and removed the blindfold, motioning for her to look up at the ceiling. Together, we watched the reflection of her pussy and ass getting fucked by me . . . by my toys . . . on my command.

Her rapid breaths were full of desire mixed with an undercurrent of anticipation. I caressed her belly, drifting my fingers over the gold chain connecting her nipple clamps. I could feel her heart racing, but I knew she trusted me.

"Do you like watching yourself getting fucked by my toys?"

"Yes, my king," she whispered.

"Does my slutty little bunny still want more?" I asked, my voice dripping with seduction.

"Y—yes," she stuttered, glancing away from her reflection. Then her eyes found my exposed cock, and widened with both fear and excitement.

"Eyes on me, Alice."

"Sorry, my king."

I gave her cheek a soft caress.

"That's better. You're learning so fast."

With a wave of my hand, I released her ankle restraints and wrist cuffs, leaving only the leash looped around her neck. With the whimsy whirls still spinning inside her holes, I gently guided her to kneel on the soft rug beside my bed. I sat on the edge of the mattress and spread my knees apart, inviting her to admire the stiff cock bobbing before her eyes.

"Does my slutty little bunny want to taste me?" I questioned, my hand gripping the leash firmly.

She didn't hesitate.

Not even a second.

"Yes, my king," she replied breathlessly, her eyes filled with lust.

"Very well," I sighed, trying my best to appear reluctant. I knew I could take it away any time I wanted.

I simply didn't *want* to.

It was still within my power to deny her. It was still my decision.

I tugged gently on the leash to guide her closer to my sex. "Show me what you're capable of."

As Alice's tongue tentatively made contact with my throbbing shaft, I couldn't help but squeeze my eyes shut and shudder at the sensation.

Fuck!

Her mouth was so hot!

So fucking wet.

She hesitated, seemingly unsure of herself, and I knew I needed to take control.

"Start by licking the underside," I instructed, my voice firm yet gentle. "Squeeze with your hands. You'll need to use both of them. And don't you dare ignore my balls."

Obediently, she followed my guidance, her tongue tracing slow, deliberate patterns along my length—each lap sending pleasure through my veins. Her little mouth opened wide, working its way around each nut like it was a delicate jewel.

As she gained confidence, her movements became more assured. Her little human hands worked my shaft while her mouth enveloped my head with such a sloppy, wet warmth that it threatened to push me over the edge.

"You're so good at this," I huffed, my fingers tightening in her hair as I guided her movements. I rewarded her by making the toys inside her wriggle and vibrate harder, eliciting a deep groan from her throat that sent vibrations through the entire length of my cock.

"Remember to breathe," I reminded her, allowing her a moment to catch her breath before resuming her task. The truth was that I needed a break so I didn't spill into her mouth. One more wanton groan from her throat and I'd be draining my balls into her. Once I was ready, I took a deep breath, then nodded at her.

"Now, take me deeper. I know you can do it. Take it *all.*"

With every inch she took into her throat, I could see Alice exploring her own desires and limits. Only hours ago she'd run screaming from me and hidden under my bed. Now she was on her knees beside it, getting fucked by my toys while sucking me off.

She'd made such progress in such a short amount of time.

Fuck . . . she was incredible.

"Focus on your breathing and relax your throat," I advised, my fingers curling around the base of my shaft as I began to thrust gently. As her gag reflex weakened, I increased the pace, my cock driving deeper with each stroke.

Alice's eager eyes began watering as she struggled to accommodate my girth and my length. Even in this mortal form, I was no comparison to the puny little human dicks she was used to. The toys inside her writhed and pulsed in time with her efforts, fueling her desire to please me.

"Almost there," I hissed, my hips snapping forward with increasing intensity. "Show me what you're capable of."

Her eyes met mine with a mix of trepidation and determination as she bobbed her head. Her wet lips kept sliding up and down my cock, oblivious to the stream of drool trickling down her chin.

Meanwhile, the whimsy whirls buried inside her wriggled and buzzed, held in place by the harness. I could feel her testing her limits and surrendering to this new side of herself—the part of her that was mine to do with as I pleased.

"You're such a good girl for me," I moaned, my breath hitching as her tongue swirled around my shaft in an impressive display of skill. "So good at giving instead of taking."

I grasped her head with both hands, trying to remind myself that I was supposed to be teaching her a lesson; one that would serve her well in the battle for Wonderland. I was supposed to be teaching her determination.

Perseverance.

Obedience.

Emotional control.

I went into this lesson expecting to throat-fuck her until she was numb, then cover her neck with a pearl necklace.

I went into this lesson determined to deny her pleasure in favor of my own.

But this wanton little slut wanted me to come . . . perhaps as much as I wanted to.

The more I felt her throat constrict around me, the more I doubted if this was the right way to teach obedience or perseverance. Every loud slurp and slap of my wet cock in her hot mouth proved how determined she actually was.

My fingers threaded through her damp blonde hair, unconsciously gathering two handfuls of it. I fucked her sloppy wet, hot mouth, wondering if she could feel the tension building within me. She nodded, her gaze never wavering for a second.

Then her eyes smiled up at me and she let out a long, deep, satisfied groan.

Without warning, I unleashed my climax into her with a roar. Thick ropes of cum splattered against her throat and filled her mouth so fast that it spilled from both corners. The excess dribbled down her chin, dripping onto her bouncing tits, making them shine in the candlelight.

This *wasn't* the plan! This spoiled little brat hadn't earned the right to *taste* me! With all my willpower, I pulled my cock out of her greedy mouth, launching another rope of cum across her belly.

Primal fury took over from there.

I shoved her to the rug, pulled both whimsy whirls out of her holes, mounted from behind, and rode her hard.

So hard.

Without mercy.

I let out a hiss of satisfaction as my cock rammed against her scorching hot, tight, slick walls. Every yelp and helpless bleat that escaped her throat only made me fuck harder.

To my surprise, the entitled brat had the nerve to reach a hand between her legs.

"What do you think you're doing?" I snarled, shoving her hand away. "*I* decide how you get to fuck!"

"Fuck me however you want!" she panted in between gasps of air. I watched in disbelief as she wiggled her hand back down between her pussy and the rug. "*I'll* decide when I get to come!"

Infuriated by her defiance, I leaned forward and grabbed her hand. Met with her resistance, I squeezed harder.

"*Ransom!*" she screamed. Her cries were so loud that at first I thought I'd accidentally broken her little hand.

"Oh *fuck!* Ransom!"

I didn't realize what was happening until I felt her cunt put my cock in a chokehold. It squeezed and tugged my shaft as she came undone all around me, screaming my name and yowling like a bandersnatch in heat.

Her hips rose up to meet each one of my thrusts, my balls slapping against her wet gash until they tightened.

Fuck! The way she screamed my name was too much.

I buried myself into the core of her heat and exploded a second time.

Her pussy was still convulsing from every direction, milking my seed, drawing it deep into her. My eyes rolled into the back of my head from the sheer force of my ecstasy. I was grateful I'd taken her from behind so she couldn't see what she'd done to me.

While continuing to thrust my last few drops into her, I opened my eyes and leaned back to admire the view. I spread her cheeks apart, watching the pearly nectar of our combined fluids leak out of her pink folds.

I hadn't planned on fucking her, but since I was already fucking her . . . I might as well keep going.

Moving quickly, I scooped her off the floor and dragged her with me onto my bed. I lay on my back and positioned her above my lap, meeting her gaze.

Then I reached between her legs and gathered as much of my seed off her as I could. I brought my fingers to her rosy lips.

"Don't waste it," I warned.

My eyes widened in fascination and delight as she complied, sucking my cum off my fingers, cleaning every last drop from them with her tongue.

I was so distracted by her mouth that I barely noticed her other hand grasp my cock. I watched her slip the head into her hungry little pussy and impale herself on me.

"You're a terrible student," I scolded, dead serious.

She shot me a coy grin.

"I know. I did better with private tutors."

"Did you ever fuck any of them?" I asked while thrusting into her delicious heat.

"Of course I did," she smirked, rolling her hips, grinding

against me, using me for her pleasure. "How do you think I got perfect grades?"

I narrowed my eyes at her.

"I'm not going to go easy on you just because I fucked you." I gazed up at the ceiling mirrors, admiring the view of her riding me on my bed. "In fact, I'll probably go harder on you."

She let out a laugh and tossed her hair over her shoulder.

"Good. I wouldn't want you to go *soft* on me."

I laughed without meaning to, then studied her in wonder.

Curiouser and curiouser . . .

To hear Callister describe this creature, I was expecting the Tweedles to bring me a demanding, unappreciative, vapid little idiot.

Not only was this Alice an incredible fuck, but she was adventurous, bold, *and* unexpectedly clever.

Heat flooded my veins, and something deep inside made me want to pull her mouth to mine. I found myself pressing my forehead against hers, staring into her eyes, but I resisted the urge to claim her mouth with my own.

I focused on fucking her instead.

"What happens when *you* bite *your* lip, my king?" she teased. "Is that my job?"

My eyes fluttered in response. I opened my mouth to reply, but I had no words. She tilted her head in silent invitation, and I took what was mine.

Our lips met in a slow, erotic dance, my tongue slipping past her parted lips to explore the depths of her clever mouth. I tasted my flavor on her, the remnants of my cum coating her tongue and mingling with the tart sweetness of her pussy.

I fucked harder, kissed harder, then slipped a finger into her slippery ass, eliciting a soft moan from her.

"Do you like that, Alice, or would you rather have the whimsy whirl instead?"

She whimpered near my ear, tightening her grip on my shoulders . . . and tightening her grip on my cock.

"You decide *how* I get fucked," she moaned, grinding harder against me, seeking friction. "I want whatever you want, my king."

My pupils dilated and my cock flexed at her obedient response. If she kept talking like this, I wasn't going to last much longer. I leaned back against my pillows and massaged her clit, watching her ride me from all the different reflections in my room.

"What I want . . . what I *really* want, is to fuck you in my true form."

Alice's body jerked as she understood what I meant.

"You mean . . . wings and all?"

I nodded my head, my wicked grin curling in satisfaction.

"Wings and all."

She slowed down her fucking and glanced down at my thick shaft, glistening in her juices.

"Eyes on me, Alice."

She did as she was told, but her expression wasn't so confident now. I knew exactly what she was thinking. She'd had that same look on her face when she saw me naked for the first time in my true form.

"Just imagine it," I began, replacing my finger with one of the metal plugs. I coaxed it into her hole, fucking her harder, applying more pressure to her swollen bud. "Imagine being licked and fucked in both holes at the same time."

Still wide-eyed, she shook her head.

"I can't."

"I'm not asking," I told her. I tossed aside the plug and slipped the smaller whimsy whirl into her ass instead. The poor thing fell forward, catching herself on my chest. "You know what I modeled this invention after, don't you?"

She shook her head, but I knew that she already knew.

"Go on, Alice. Say it out loud."

She hesitated, pressing her lips together. I turned up the dial and let the toy explore the depths of her ass while she rode my shaft.

"Your demon cock?"

"Yes." I licked my thumb and brought it back to her hard nub. "Now imagine a tongue licking you while I ride you."

"Oh, fuck . . . " she moaned.

"Exactly."

I removed the gold clamps and set them aside, then sucked a nipple into my mouth. Her arms clutched tighter around me as she let out a muffled squeal.

"You're going to come again," I ordered. "You're going to come all over my cock for me, aren't you?"

"Yes, my king," she sighed in my ear, panting harder.

I watched her face twist in pleasure as the toy sped up. My thrusts grew deeper. Faster. I removed my thumb, grinding even harder against her clit. I heard the familiar hitch in her breath that told me her body was coiling, ready to spring.

"That's it. Come for me, Alice," I softly urged, my voice low. "Keep your eyes open. I want to see your face when I come inside you."

"I'm so close . . . Oh, Ransom . . . " she gasped, fighting to keep her eyes open.

Fuck—

I held perfectly still, but hearing her say my name made me completely lose it.

My climax burned up through me like an all-consuming eruption, bursting into her cunt, flooding her with my essence. I watched her brows furrow in wonder, knowing that she could feel my hot seed blasting her insides.

"Come for me right now!" I growled as I started fucking her again. I pushed the toy in her ass to full speed.

Alice gasped and shuddered as she came again, harder than

before. I watched the waves of pleasure wash over her until they were dripping down my balls.

And as I felt her tremors ripple and constrict all around me, squeezing me, sucking my passion into her core, she never looked away from me.

Not once.

I should've praised her for it . . .

I should've congratulated myself for it . . .

But everything about this evening felt too good to be true.

I didn't trust it.

I didn't trust *her*.

Even worse—I didn't trust myself.

Especially not when my cock was buried in her slick, hot folds.

I let out a sigh and pulled her with me down into the pillows, resting her head against my chest, stroking her silky hair. It felt so good, so right, and yet, I was painfully aware that I'd let her get exactly what she wanted without any sort of punishment.

I'd let her say my name. More than once. And I'd let it pass without reprimand.

I'd let her take her pleasure.

I'd let her take mine as well.

I stared up at our reflection, remembering the last time I'd let a woman take something from me.

It had cost me dearly . . .

And all of Wonderland was paying for it.

I glanced down at my pinky ring, guilt and shame taunting me, reminding me of what a fool I'd been. What a fool I still *was*.

Whatever I'd just started with Alice, it had to end here.

I kept stroking her hair with one hand, and wound the excess length of her leash around the other. I wouldn't let myself fall asleep until my pet was locked safe in her cage.

She nuzzled against my chest and let out a contented sigh,

making me wonder if I was being too cautious. Would it really be so awful to let this exquisite creature sleep in my bed?

I didn't know. That was the problem.

Callister was right about one thing—this Alice was completely different from all the others.

She was a weakness.

The same kind of weakness that put my friends Hatter and Chess at risk. I hoped that wherever they were, they were safe.

CHAPTER
SEVEN
CHESS

Chained in the Red Queen's dungeon, Hatter sat beside me in our shared cell, his eyes filled with madness and despair. Callister had been taken away by the Red Queen's guards earlier, and we both knew what awaited him. It was only a matter of time before he'd be tortured for information.

Information about Alice.

I had a plan, but I didn't dare say it out loud until I knew I could put it into action. It was dangerous, reckless even, but it was our only chance at freedom.

As the minutes ticked by, I felt my demon powers slowly returning. Magic coursed through me, growing stronger with each passing moment. The sensation was like a warm embrace, surging through my veins, reigniting the demon within.

My heart raced with anticipation as I realized that the cold metal chains binding me to the damp stone wall had stopped chafing my skin.

Good.

I was back to healing myself on demand.

Now it was time for action.

Taking a deep breath, I focused on my truest, purest form, a creature that belonged neither to the earth nor the air. I wasn't born from flesh and bone. I wasn't born of water or fire.

Cheshire Cat demons belonged to the ether.

Channeling all my newfound strength into freeing myself, I lifted my arms and watched the chains fall through my semi-transparent wrists. With a resounding clang, the metal cuffs hit the filthy stone floor, freeing me from their oppressive hold.

"Curiouser and curiouser," Hatter breathed, staring at me in wonder. "Does this mean you're back to full strength?"

"Yes. Are you ready for a little chaos, my friend?" I asked, a wicked grin on my face.

"Always," he responded. His blue eye began to gleam with excitement.

"Stay quiet," I warned as I floated onto my feet. "Freeing you won't be nearly as easy."

I focused my energy, feeling the demon magic pulse and grow stronger within me. I stared at the metal bars of our cell, then stepped forward. Their coolness made me shiver as I passed through them and reappeared on the opposite side. I quickly took my human form, the one made of flesh and blood.

Just as I'd hoped, my sudden appearance caught the attention of a nearby guard who withdrew his sword and approached, his eyes narrowed in confusion.

"Hello there." I gave him a polite wave, showing him I was completely unarmed. I had no need for weapons.

I was the weapon.

"How did you get out?" he asked, glancing at the locked metal gate and then back at me.

"I could tell you, but then I'd have to kill you," I purred, grinning wide.

He aimed his sword at me while reaching for his keys, then opened the lock on the gate.

"You'd better get back in there before I kill you first," he ordered.

I merely shook my head.

"That's not going to happen."

The shadows around us swirled around me as my body shifted into its beast form, until I was a hulking, demonic creature made of fur and fangs and massive claws. I reveled in watching the guard's eyes widen in horror as he realized what I was.

"I'm a Cheshire Cat demon . . . that's how I escaped," I hissed. "And now I have to kill you."

"Wha—what the—" he stammered, but before he could finish his sentence, I lunged forward, my giant claws slashing through the air and slicing his throat wide open. Blood sprayed all over my chest and neck, then against the cold stone walls as he crumpled to the ground, lifeless.

"That's a terrible paint job, Chess," Hatter quipped as he motioned to the red blood spattered on the wall. In seconds, I'd shifted back to my human form, pristine and clean. I snatched the set of keys from the dead guard's hand, then quickly freed Hatter from his shackles.

"Take off your clothes," I told him, nodding towards the guard's bloody uniform. Hatter's eyes brightened with glee.

"What's this? Is the cat feeling frisky?" he laughed as he unbuttoned his tattered shirt. "But if you insist . . . "

"I'm trying to help you escape, you nitwit earthbound fae," I retorted with a light growl.

Together, we stripped the corpse of his armor and wiped it clean, then redressed him in Hatter's clothes. He busied himself with positioning the dead man's body to look like he was sleeping while I made the bloody mess in the hall vanish.

Damn, it felt good to be back to my old self.

"Let's find Callister," I said, my voice low and urgent. Hatter nodded in agreement, his eyes filled with determination.

I made myself invisible, existing completely in the ether as we made our way out of the dungeon and through the castle. Nobody stopped us once—a single guard walking with purpose was almost as invisible as I was.

Being a demon with the power to appear and reappear at will, and to move through walls, I'd explored the Red Queen's castle countless times. I knew my way around. I relied on my heightened sense of smell to track Callister's scent. It led us straight to the throne room, a place that was simultaneously opulent yet dripping in decay—a testament to the Red Queen's twisted reign of oppression.

The air was heavy with the scent of death. Here and there were large basins piled with severed limbs, the rotting flesh crawling with worms. Large, fat, carnivorous flies buzzed around, drunk on the never-ending source of food. Mold and mildew clung to the walls in broad, uneven patches of black and green.

A massive tent of glistening silver spiderwebs hung from the vaulted ceiling, trapping the most careless flies. Mushrooms and fungus of every shape and color sprouted out of every nook and cranny. Some were perfectly shaped for sitting on, but nobody in the room would dare. Not in the Red Queen's throne room.

The windows were made of red stained glass, depicting gruesome scenes from the Red Queen's countless victories in battle. The queen plunging a spear into a bandersnatch. The queen slicing through a colony of glitterblooms. The queen standing with one foot on the decapitated head of an Alice.

That last one never happened.

But the Red Queen wasn't fond of the truth. Her vanity wouldn't allow her to see it. And her subjects' fear of her wouldn't allow them to correct her.

She truly believed her own lies.

Long red velvet banners hung heavily from the walls, their once vibrant colors now faded and stained with age. They were embroidered with the queen's sigil of a heart. Smaller hearts had been embroidered in black all along the banners, but something was off about them. Dark red shriveled objects had been pinned to most of the smaller hearts. I squinted my eyes and looked closer.

It couldn't be . . .

Yet it definitely was.

They were hearts. I could only hope that they'd been removed after the poor soul was beheaded, and not before.

"Stay quiet and observe," I instructed Hatter as he took his place among the guards lining the back wall. He blended in seamlessly, his eyes scanning the room for any sign of our friend.

"Where is that damned caterpillar?" I muttered under my breath, my frustration building as the minutes ticked by. But I couldn't risk exposing us until I was certain Callister was here. *Patience, Chess*, I reminded myself, even as every fiber of my being screamed at me to tear this wretched place apart.

I floated through the air undetected, scanning the voices of the people in the room, hoping for gossip or any useful information.

Nothing.

I drifted back to the wall where I'd left my friend.

"Find him yet?" Hatter whispered, his voice barely audible over the din of the throne room.

"No," I replied, gritting my teeth. "But he has to be here somewhere. I can smell him."

"Focus, Chess," Hatter urged, his tone laced with concern. "We can't afford to make a single mistake."

"Trust me, I know," I snapped, my patience wearing thin.

Then, at last, I caught another whiff of Callister's scent—it was faint but unmistakable. Relief surged through me, quickly followed by a renewed sense of urgency.

"Over there," I murmured, spotting Callister bound and awaiting interrogation. Hatter took his place along the back wall, blending in seamlessly with the other guards as he observed in silence.

From my invisible vantage point, I studied the room, my heart pounding with trepidation. We had found Callister, but our mission was far from over. We still needed to free him from the clutches of the Red Queen and ensure Alice's safety.

"Chess," Hatter whispered urgently, his voice barely audible. "We need a plan!"

"We'll wait for the right moment," I replied, my mind racing with possibilities. "Then we strike. I'll give you a sign."

"What's the sign?"

"You'll know it when you see it."

Hatter cast me a serious frown.

"Can it be purple?"

"What?"

Hatter rolled his eyes at me. Meanwhile, I wanted to choke him for being such an infuriating fae.

"If I don't know what the sign is going to be, can you at least make it purple so I know it's meant for me?"

"Yes," I hissed through clenched teeth. "I'll make it purple so you know it's for you."

I promptly floated away before I was tempted to throttle him. While Hatter's particular brand of madness was endearing most of the time, this was not one of them.

But he was all I had right now. No matter what it took, we would save Callister and protect Alice.

Wonderland's future depended on it.

The Red Queen entered the throne room, and even in my invisible state, I could feel the weight of her presence. Her beauty was both enchanting and terrifying, a deadly combination that left many trembling in her wake. She wore a provocative, skin-tight red gown with a plunging neckline that accentuated her full breasts, and slits on either side that revealed her long legs. Her ruby red hair cascaded down her back like a waterfall of blood, and her sharp, pointy blood-red nails threatened to pierce through anyone who dared to defy her.

As she moved, the gold ring on her finger captured the light, casting sinister glimmers across the room. Every step she took exuded confidence and power, while her facial expressions oscillated between cruel amusement and unbridled fury.

She used to be so beautiful, so absolutely stunning. Now her face was a mask of cold fury, and her eyes burned with a barely contained rage. I watched as she settled onto her throne, a predatory smile playing on her lips.

"Bring forth the criminals," she commanded, her voice sending a chill of silence throughout the room.

A group of trembling prisoners was led forward, their faces etched with fear and despair.

As they were lined up before the Red Queen, an official began to read out their charges.

"Sir Reginald Pembrook, accused of sneezing without covering his mouth in the presence of royalty."

"Miss Marigold Winters, charged with laughing at a joke not approved by the court jester."

"Mr. Bartholomew Finch, whose crimes include, but are not limited to: failure to properly groom a Jabberwocky, unlicensed use of shrinking potions, and conspiring to steal the Red Queen's tarts."

The prisoners stared in disbelief, mouths agape at the ridiculousness of their supposed crimes. I could feel the tension in the room rise, and I could hardly believe my ears. The absurdity of the charges was astonishing, but the fear in the eyes of the condemned spoke volumes about the Red Queen's iron grip over Wonderland.

"Enough!" she snapped, her words slicing through the air like a blade. "I have heard enough."

"Wait!" Sir Reginald cried out, his voice shaking with terror. "Please, Your Majesty, we're innocent! We've done nothing wrong!"

"Silence!" she roared, her eyes flashing with anger. "You dare to question my judgment? You dare to defy your queen?"

"No, Your Majesty," he replied, cowering before her.

The queen sat still for a moment, glaring at the prisoners, tapping her fingernails on the arm of her chair. Meanwhile, everyone in the room held their breath.

Maybe today would be different.

The Red Queen let out a bored sigh.

"Off with their heads," she ordered nonchalantly, playing with one of her razor-sharp nails.

"No, please!" Sir Reginald cried out, but his plea fell on deaf ears as he and the others were dragged away. I could see the color drain from their faces, their eyes wide with fear as they realized the full extent of the Red Queen's cruelty.

Hatter and I continued to watch, our resolve hardening like steel, as the Red Queen reveled in her power. But even as we waited for our chance to free our friend, I couldn't shake the nagging feeling that time was running out for Callister, for Alice, and for Wonderland itself.

We needed to act, and fast.

The Red Queen's guards marched into the throne room, their boots echoing loudly against the marble floor, their faces completely blank. They gripped Callister tightly by his arms, dragging him toward the grotesque seat of power at the center of the cavernous space. His tattoos seemed to squirm beneath his tight bindings as he clenched his jaw, defiant even in captivity.

To my surprise, Dinah elegantly stepped forward and curt-seyed for the queen before taking her place beside the throne. My stomach turned as my fears were confirmed—The queen's loyal servant and Alice's assistant were one and the same . . . and she'd been working against us all along.

"Ah, there you are," the Red Queen said, looking down her nose at Callister. "I've been expecting you."

"Really now?" he spat, venom dripping from his words. "I

must be quite the catch."

"You're a slippery little worm, but I've finally got my hooks in you," the Red Queen replied with a cruel smile. She leaned forward, her fingers tapping the armrest of her throne. "You're about to become very useful to me, my dear."

With a flick of her wrist, she gestured for her guards to release Callister in front of her. She rose from her throne and sauntered around him like a predator stalking its prey, stopping to admire his ink-covered body with a twisted grin.

"Such lovely artwork," she commented, her sharp nails grazing his skin, leaving thin trails of blood in their wake. "It would be such a shame if anything were to . . . mar its beauty."

Callister's eyes narrowed, but he refused to give her the satisfaction of a reaction. "What do you want from me, Your Majesty?"

"Oh, Callister," the Red Queen murmured, her voice dripping with venomous honey. "I've heard that you know *exactly* where Alice is. My spies are everywhere, you see." She glanced at Dinah and gave her a sickly-sweet smile. "And I will find her. You can either make it easier on yourself or suffer the consequences."

Her psychopathic tendencies were on full display, her narcissistic need for control evident in every word she spoke. The room seemed to tremble under the weight of her irrational fury, and I could only imagine what horrors she'd unleash upon Callister if he refused to cooperate.

"Your Majesty, I have no idea where Alice is," Callister replied, the words slipping off his tongue like silk.

"Is that so?" The Red Queen's eyes narrowed, and she rose from her throne. "Well, then, I suppose I'll have to help you remember where you left her."

She gestured to one of her guards, who approached with a cart. It was filled with a menacing collection of torture instruments. Whips, chains, and various sharp implements gleamed in the dim light, casting twisted shadows across the walls.

Callister's eyes sparkled with a dark hunger as he licked his lips, sizing up the instruments that were meant to break him. I found it both disturbing and fascinating; this man, who enjoyed pain, was about to face the Red Queen's wrath.

"Choose your poison, dear Callister," she teased, her grin wicked. "Or perhaps you'd prefer something more . . . creative? I'm sure my guards can come up with something new and exciting just for you."

"Your threats don't scare me," Callister replied in a bored tone. "I don't know where Alice is."

"Very well." She sighed theatrically, as if disappointed by his stubbornness. She turned to her guards and snapped her fingers. "Begin."

The tension in the throne room was almost unbearable. I could feel Hatter's eyes on me, urging me to act, but I knew we had to be patient. We couldn't risk the Red Queen discovering our presence, not when so much was at stake. The Red Queen's wrath would be our chance to turn the tide—but only if we played our cards right.

As the first strike of the whip connected with Callister's back, I braced myself for his inevitable scream of pain.

But it never came.

Instead, he let out a guttural moan, one that held an unmistakable hint of pleasure. His eyes fluttered closed, and a small smirk played on his lips. He seemed to relish the pain, as if it were an old friend.

"More," he whispered, his voice dripping with perverse eagerness. Whispers rose up all throughout the room.

The Red Queen's eyes widened in disgust before narrowing into a furious glare. "Make it hurt more! I want him begging for mercy!"

She motioned towards her guards, who hesitated only for a moment before unleashing their fury upon Callister.

"Harder," he gasped, arching his back to meet every hit.

"You'll have to do better than that if you want me to remember something I don't know."

The room echoed with the sounds of their whips cracking against his flesh, each strike more vicious than the last. But instead of breaking, Callister laughed, his arousal evident as each blow seemed to fuel his desire.

The torture continued, much to everyone's horror and Callister's delight. The guards used every instrument they had: knives that sliced through his flesh like butter, red-hot pokers that seared his skin, and all the while, Callister embraced the pain, his face contorted in a perverse mix of agony and ecstasy.

"Is that all you've got?" he taunted, smirking at the Red Queen. "I've had worse on a slow afternoon."

"You sick, twisted creature!" she finally screamed, her face twisted in fury.

In the stunned silence that followed, the atmosphere in the throne room grew heavy with tension. Nobody dared to move or speak as the Red Queen paced back and forth, trying to contain her anger.

Suddenly Dinah gestured to the guards, their eyes wide with confusion and fear. "Use your imagination to create something more painful!"

Two guards shared a look, then one of them conjured one more object onto the cart—a whip covered in long, razor-sharp thorns.

As I watched, invisible and horrified, I couldn't help but feel the tension in the room grow thick and suffocating. The other prisoners shifted uncomfortably in their chains, trying to avoid looking at Callister's mangled body. Even the guards paused in between blows, glancing nervously at each other, their hands slick with sweat as they hesitated between tormenting Callister further and fearing the Red Queen's wrath.

In the midst of this madness, something caught my eye—a small, shiny object that slipped from Callister's pocket and clattered onto the cold stone floor. It was a gold chip, embossed with the unmistakable logo of Ransom's casino, the Rabbit Hole.

The sound of the chip hitting the floor seemed to echo throughout the throne room, capturing everyone's attention with its cheerful metallic chime. The stunned silence that followed was almost deafening.

The Red Queen's gaze snapped to the chip, her eyes glittering with a dangerous curiosity.

"Guards!" she bellowed, her voice like thunder. "Cease your torture . . . for now."

The guards immediately stopped their assault on Callister, who slumped forward in his chains, panting heavily. Blood dripped from his countless wounds, but still, that twisted smile remained on his lips.

Meanwhile, Dinah retrieved the gold chip and handed it to the queen.

"Tell me, dear Callister," the Red Queen continued, her voice low and menacing, "have you recently been to the Rabbit Hole? Did you bring Alice there?"

Callister's head lifted, a smirk playing on his lips despite the pain he had just endured. He remained silent, refusing to answer her.

"Tell me!" I could see her frustration mounting as she glared at Callister, waiting for a response that wouldn't come.

"Answer me!" she demanded, her fists curled and blood-red nails digging into her palms.

Callister said nothing, his jaw clenched tight as beads of sweat trickled down his face. But it was enough; the Red Queen now had a lead, and it wouldn't be long before she followed it straight to Alice.

The Red Queen's fury was palpable as she stared Callister down. "Fine. Have it your way, you pathetic *worm*," she hissed, her fingers tapping impatiently on the armrest of her throne.

"Dinah, pack my things. We're paying a visit to an old friend of mine."

Dinah nodded obediently, her eyes betraying no emotion as she turned to leave. The Red Queen stalked out of the throne room, her gown trailing behind her like a river of blood.

The guards began to escort Callister away, and I knew this was my moment to act.

Still invisible, I focused all of my energy, then leapt up and pounced on the nearest banner hanging from the ceiling. I pulled it down, then jumped to the next one, and the next, until the heavy, moldy banners covered in rotting hearts had buried a third of the queen's courtiers.

With all my power, I flipped the giant basins of decaying limbs, showering the people with festering, putrid, worm-infested flesh.

And I made sure all of it was purple.

To my relief, Hatter seized the opportunity in the midst of the chaos and commotion, grabbing Callister by his chains and leading him away from the other guards.

"Follow us," I whispered in Callister's ear. He blinked in surprise, but he didn't hesitate to walk with Hatter. While chaos played out in the Red Queen's absence, we slipped away effortlessly from the throne room and into the dark corridors of the castle.

I led us to the best exit that I knew of, a root cellar in the kitchens. I knew there was a set of doors that led to the Wickedwood Forest, and the three of us soon found ourselves standing in dark shade of the moldy trees.

"I'm actually quite impressed with you," Callister huffed as Hatter let go of him.

"I had help," he said as I reappeared by his side. "Seems like we got away clean."

I was so concerned with freeing Callister from his chains that it took me a moment to register his injuries. Every last inch of his body was cut or bruised, and all of it covered in his purple blood. Even his tattoos were impossible to decipher, they were so mangled and torn.

"Callister, are you alright?" Hatter asked softly from behind his armor.

"I'm fine," he replied with a smirk, although it didn't quite reach his eyes.

"You're a mess," I argued.

"I've been in tighter spots before."

I couldn't shake off a nagging feeling that we hadn't gotten away as cleanly as it seemed. Hatter, on the other hand, appeared confident in our escape.

"Piece of cake," he muttered under his breath, a smirk tugging at the corner of his lips.

A low growl resonated in my chest. "Don't be so certain, Hatter. We're not out of the woods yet."

Hatter snapped his fingers and the armor disappeared, replaced by his tattered clothes and top hat.

"Have you looked around?" he asked, gesturing to the rotting trees that surrounded us. "We're in the woods, and yet we're out of it!"

"Don't jinx us," I hissed, but it was too late.

As if to confirm my suspicions, a chorus of howls from abyssal hounds spilled out of the castle. I could sense the bloodthirsty creatures closing in on us, drawn by the scent of our trail.

"Ah, *now* we're fucked," Hatter said with a maniacal laugh.

"Stay focused, Chess," Callister advised, seeing my thoughts drift towards darker paths. "We'll find a way out of this. We always do."

Judging by the howls, there were at least half a dozen abyssal hounds coming for us.

We were in no shape to fight them together.

Hatter was in no state of mind to defend himself, and thanks to the Red Queen, Callister was already beaten to a pulp.

If we were going to survive, I'd have to take care of this myself.

"Well, my brothers, it's been lovely knowing you," Hatter said, wagging his finger at me.

Tempted as I was to break it, I knew he'd need it.

I couldn't take on all of the monsters by myself.

But I could *become* a monster.

My eyes began to glow as my human body morphed into as massive of a Cheshire Cat beast as I could muster. My sharp, deadly claws dug into the forest floor as I crouched down beside my friends.

"Get on," I commanded, my voice guttural and filled with urgency. Without hesitation, Callister and Hatter clambered onto my back, gripping my thick fur tightly as I took off at break-neck speed.

The abyssal hounds' snarls and barks drew closer to my heels, but I didn't falter. My heart raced, adrenaline pumping through my veins as I prepared for the inevitable confrontation. One by one, I tore through the pack of hellish creatures, slashing and ripping their throats apart with ferocious intensity.

"Is that all of them?" I asked as I continued to run through the trees.

"Should be," Callister replied from my back, his breath ragged from the effort.

"Chess, where are we going?" Hatter asked frantically, his eyes scanning our surroundings for any sign of danger.

"Rabbit Hole," I replied, my voice strained from the effort of carrying them both. But I didn't dare stop running.

We needed to reach Ransom before the Red Queen did.

The fate of Wonderland depended on it.

EIGHT

ALICE

The memory of Ransom's touch lingered on my skin, a phantom caress that danced up and down my curves. I don't think he'd planned to fuck me last night, but *damn* . . .

I needed what he was dishing out.

I'd played him like a fucking violin. I let him think I didn't know anything about sucking dick. It was so satisfying, so hot, listening to him give me orders like I didn't have a clue.

Of *course* I had a clue.

Being outstanding at blowjobs was how I got rich boys to buy me whatever I wanted in high school and college. It wasn't that I couldn't afford those things. I totally could. I only did it because I didn't want to spend my money when I could spend theirs.

And spend it, I did.

Guys were like tile floors—lay 'em right the first time, and you could walk all over them forever.

So when I gobbled up Ransom's huge cock and started humming while he deep-throated me, I knew I was going to get exactly what I wanted. I'd stroked his ego just as much as I stroked his cock.

In return, Ransom had brought me to the height of pleasure again and again, pushing me to places I didn't know even existed. But then he ordered me to look at him while I came, and I started to come undone.

In that moment when our eyes met, something shifted between us. It shifted in *me*, anyway. It felt dangerously close to catching feelings.

Did he feel it too?

Could a demon even *have* feelings?

I yawned and opened my eyes, expecting to see his hulking, muscular body resting beside mine.

Instead, I saw black metal bars.

I scrambled to sit up and immediately smacked my head against cold, hard metal.

"Motherfucker!"

I winced at the pain and rubbed my head, my grogginess quickly replaced by confusion and rising anger. Ransom had caged me like an animal at the foot of his bed!

What the hell was this bullshit?

Any warmth I'd felt for him instantly evaporated, replaced by simmering resentment.

I heard him laugh nearby. Then I watched him slip out of bed and into his black robe and slippers.

"What the fuck is this?" I spat, narrowing my eyes at him. Ransom merely smirked, unfazed by my bitterness.

"Good morning, Alice," he replied, his tone infuriatingly nonchalant. "Did you sleep well?"

"Like you actually give a shit!" I snarked, propping myself up on an elbow. I banged on the bars with my other fist, the metallic clang echoing through the bedroom. "I have to pee! Let me out of here!"

"Ah, but where would be the fun in that?" Ransom mused, stepping closer to the cage. His gaze locked onto mine, a predatory glint in his eyes. "You see, my pet, last night was . . . unexpected, but it doesn't change anything between us. You're still here to be trained. Pets sleep in cages, not in their master's bed."

"Here's a newsflash, asshole!" I snapped, my anger boiling over. "You're not supposed to fuck your pets!"

"Perhaps not," he admitted with a wry grin. "But I'm very glad you're accepting the fact that you *are* my pet."

"Fuck you," I muttered under my breath, knowing full well that Ransom would hear me.

"Bunny, we've already done that," he replied with mock sweetness, causing me to scowl at him.

Deep inside, a part of me wondered if he might be right.

Was I his pet?

His slutty little bunny?

He drove me crazy, and yet, not all of it was the bad kind of crazy. This dark Wonderland was changing me, stripping away my old beliefs and leaving me questioning myself. And in Ransom's hands, I couldn't help but wonder what kind of creature I would become.

He conjured a riding crop into his hand and opened the cage door, but I didn't budge.

"I'm not getting out until you put that away," I snapped at him.

"I've had enough of your insolence," he growled, his patience wearing thin. He reached in and yanked me out by my arm. "If you insist on behaving like a stubborn mule, I'll treat you like one."

"Let go of me!" I yelled, but he didn't relent. Instead, he bent me over the edge of his bed and brought the riding crop down on my bare ass with a sharp crack. The sting was intense, and I couldn't help but cry out.

"Today's lesson, Alice: humility," he said coolly, landing another blow with the crop. My body tensed, anticipating the next strike, but it never came.

Part of me was praying for him to sink his cock into me. If he was going to treat me like a stubborn mule, the least he could do was ride me.

"Get on all fours and crawl to your meal," Ransom commanded, pointing at a golden bowl on the floor across the room. I hesitated, my inner pride at odds with my hunger, but another sharp swat from the crop made the decision for me. I lowered myself to my hands and knees, feeling humiliated as I crawled toward the dish.

"Please, my king . . . at least let me tie back my hair," I begged, but Ransom shook his head.

"Animals don't have the luxury of such considerations," he said dismissively. "You'll eat off the floor, just like they do."

My face flushed with shame and anger, but I knew better than to argue with him. He'd been so different last night . . . cuddling me in his arms after rocking my world. He'd been so careful with me . . . so thoughtful.

I must've been dreaming.

Maybe it was just a dream within a dream.

It had to still be a dream, because even as a kid, I never ate out of a dish on the floor.

As I dipped my head to eat, strands of hair fell into the bowl, getting sticky and dirty. Some of it mixed with the food and got into my mouth, making the experience even more degrading.

"Remember this humiliation, Alice," Ransom told me as I choked down the meal, trying to ignore the texture of my own hair caught in my mouth. "It's important for you to learn that you're not above anyone else. You need to develop a strong work ethic and understand the value of perseverance."

I swallowed the last of the disgusting meal, clenching my fists in frustration. But I didn't look at him. I stared at the shiny black and gold tiles beneath me.

"Fine," I spat. I pulled my hair out of my mouth and wiped my lips with the back of my hand. "Lesson learned. Are you satisfied, my king?"

"Hardly," he replied with a wicked grin. "But it's a start."

Once I had finished eating, Ransom gave me a bathroom break and then put me back in my cage. Even though I was angry at him, I was lonely when he left.

Hours passed by in miserable silence.

Nobody walked past the hall, nobody came by to tidy up the room . . . not that it needed it. There was no music, no windows to look out of. Just candles that burned forever.

The silence of the room weighed heavily on me as thoughts of the next Bunny Bondage Game gnawed at my mind. My body still ached from last night's pillow fight and subsequent fuckfest. I couldn't help but wonder what other humiliating trials awaited me.

After spending the whole day in my cage, Ransom returned to give me another bathroom break. He didn't speak to me at all.

"What happened between this morning and last night?" I asked while I sat on the toilet. "How did you go from snuggling with me in bed to locking me in a cage? I know it wasn't anything I did, so it has to be you."

I could practically hear him glowering at me from the other side of the door.

"Hurry up. The next challenge begins shortly."

I frowned as I flushed the toilet and stood up. Thanks to the pillow fight and the sexual acrobatics from last night, every muscle in my body ached and burned.

"What's the next challenge?"

No reply.

I stood on the other side of the door and waited.

And waited.

And waited some more.

"Are you finished?" Ransom finally growled, and I found myself smiling.

"That depends. What's the next challenge?"

"I don't have time for this," he warned. "Come out *now*."

"No."

I waited for him to keep arguing with me, but Ransom was a demon. He didn't fuck around with belligerent mortals.

There was a loud cracking of wood and a groan of twisting metal as he pulled the door off its hinges and threw it on the floor. It shattered into a cloud of glittery black diamond dust.

Then he stepped through the cloud, his rage tempered by years and years of wisdom and experience.

His hands were on me in an instant, binding my wrists behind my back. Ignoring my protests, he put a different version of my bunny mask over my face . . . this one only had openings for my eyes and my nose. My mouth was covered, my lips brushing against rough metal.

I stole a glance in the mirror. It was a fucking *zipper*!

"You asshole!" I shouted, but it came out more like, "Oooaaaooohhh!"

He grasped my jaw in his hands and looked down his nose at me. I knew by the look in his eyes that whatever had made him hold me close last night was gone.

"I told you not to waste my time, pet . . . "

Then he dragged me by my leash down to the Rabbit Hole, handing me off to the Tweedles the second they appeared.

I didn't know what his problem was, but I was glad to be rid of him.

The casino was alive with the cacophony of hedonistic pleasure. The air buzzed with the heated moans and soft sighs of the club guests, mingling with the sultry music that played from a hidden source.

Chains clinked as they hoisted bodies into midair, holding them in place. Their metallic chimes harmonized with the sharp slaps and smacks of impact play that echoed throughout the dimly lit room. The scent of leather, clean sweat, and filthy sex permeated the atmosphere, equally intoxicating and overwhelming.

Even though it was also a casino, there wasn't much gambling going on. Games at the tables had either finished early or been put on hold, most likely because everyone wanted to bet on the Bunny Bondage Games instead. The giant wrestling ring was gone, replaced by a simple black platform. Tonight's crowd was even bigger than the one from last night's pillow fight.

"Welcome back, ladies and gentlemen, to the second night of the Bunny Bondage Games," Ransom announced from the platform, his voice dripping with cool authority. The club guests roared with anticipation, their excitement palpable. "Tonight's game is a new one, yet it's one you all know and love—musical chairs!"

A dubious look took over my face.

Sure, it sounded innocent enough, but Ransom was a freak. I knew better than to take anything in his club at face value.

"However," he continued, his grin widening, "there's a twist. Each chair has been . . . *modified*, for your entertainment and for our competitors' as well."

I swallowed nervously, my heart pounding in anticipation. What could he possibly have in store for us this time?

As he spoke, the house lights went out and a pink spotlight slowly illuminated the platform that held nothing but a huge circle of black chairs. Two referees were walking around to each and every chair with what looked like a small pail and a basting brush.

I squinted my eyes in the dark room, taking a few steps to get a better look at what they were basting. My cheeks flushed with humiliation as gasps echoed throughout the room. The thought of being forced to participate in such a degrading act made my stomach churn.

I wasn't surprised.

I was fucking *dumbstruck*.

Every chair was outfitted with a different dildo protruding from the seat.

Some were small and non-threatening. Some were lean and long, while others were short and thick. A number of them were slick and smooth, although there were a few that looked knobby and rough. There wasn't a big enough basting brush or pail of lube to make *any* of them feel good.

The longer I looked, the more I noticed that a disturbing percentage of them were clearly *not* modeled on human male anatomy.

A shudder of fascination and revulsion ran through me as I studied the various tentacles and knots. Then a pearly blue one with shiny, wet scales caught my eye.

Was it supposed to be a merman schlong?

"Allow me to explain the rules," Ransom said, relishing the number of bets that were already being placed. "Music will play. When the music stops, our lovely bunnies must claim a chair and sit down. Yes, *all* the way down . . . "

He let the words hang in the air, sending my stomach into knots while the crowd whistled and cheered.

I knew a little about BDSM. Couldn't Ransom have chosen a spanking competition, or rope-tying, or something like that? Why did he have to choose dildo musical chairs when I still ached from him fucking me?

It was almost like he *wanted* me to fail.

I'd show him.

"As a safety precaution to my bunnies, the modifications will be replaced between every round," he went on. "Failure for a bunny to completely sit in a chair when the music stops will result in disqualification. Alright, my pets, are you ready to play?"

His loyal squad of sex bunnies swarmed onto the stage, eyeing up the different dildos, trying to find the ones they'd rather sit down on. The Tweedles unlocked my wrist restraints, but I hesitated to move, dread settling in my gut like a stone. What choice did I have?

I was going for the merman schlong.

The glare of the spotlights blinded me as I stepped onto the stage, the thudding bass of the music vibrating in my chest. I glanced around, spotting the familiar faces of my competition: Dickface sneered at me with contempt, while Trippy's eyes flashed with malice.

Caramel, however, gave me an encouraging smile and whispered, "Good luck" as she took her place in line not far from me.

"Ready?" Ransom shouted to the audience, his eyes never connecting with mine. "Let the games begin!"

The music started, a surreal, haunting tune that seemed to mock my predicament. I moved cautiously around the circle of chairs, eyeing the other contestants warily. We were all trapped in this perverse competition, but I couldn't afford to let my guard down.

My body moved in time with the rhythm, anticipation tightening in my chest as I waited for the signal to dive for a chair. Each brief pause in the music was a cruel taunt, sending us darting towards the dildos, only to be denied when the melody resumed. With every near-miss, I clenched my teeth and steeled myself for the next round.

"Hey, new girl," Caramel whispered, her eyes filled with concern as we circled the chairs. "Watch your back. A lot of the others want nothing more than to see you fail. I think they're planning something to take you out."

"Thanks," I replied, trying to keep my tone light despite the weight of her words. "I'll be careful."

The music stopped abruptly, and I lunged for the nearest chair, my heart racing as I shoved a smaller girl out of the way. The slippery dildo loomed below me, and as I lowered myself onto it, I winced at the discomfort. I tried to focus on the memory of Ransom's touch from the previous night, letting the lingering pleasure soothe the pain as it stretched my tender insides. Even dripping with lube, it took some effort.

One female bunny was immediately disqualified for not

finding a chair. At least four more bunnies were eliminated for not touching their ass cheeks to the chair seat. One guy was having such a hard time with the bumpy knobby cock that he finally shook his head and gave up.

The crowd roared with laughter at the spectacle.

As the second round played out, I tried to focus on the beat of the music, but my thoughts were consumed by the mounting pressure of the competition. I couldn't help but feel exposed and vulnerable, knowing that every move I made was under scrutiny. Trippy and Dickface both seemed to revel in my discomfort, their smirks only fueling my determination to prove them wrong.

Round after round, we repeated the process, each time removing one less chair than the number of remaining bunnies. With every cock I impaled myself with, my body ached, my vaginal walls protesting as I continued to push through the discomfort. But I refused to give in. I wasn't going to let Ransom or his twisted games break me.

My heart raced as the music played, knowing that one misstep could mean the end of my participation. And yet, despite my determination, I couldn't help but feel a flicker of hope that maybe, just *maybe*, I could win this fucked up event. I just had to work smarter, not harder.

As the next round of musical chairs began, I knew I needed a new strategy. My soreness from last night's trip to Poundtown was only making things worse. With each step I took, I could feel the burn and ache between my legs.

The thing about pain is that it's *sooo* fucking close to pleasure.

It was time to give things a little push in the other direction.

Closing my eyes, I tried to block out the sounds of the casino and the jeers from the spectators. Instead, I replayed the memory of Ransom's hands on my body, his lips against my clit, and the way I'd made him completely lose control.

I thought about the sound me made when he came inside me,

the heat I felt when he came inside me, riding me like the stubborn mule he said I was. The sound of his pleasure made me want to do that to him over and over.

I'd make him fucking *beg* for my pussy.

Then I thought of the way he'd kissed me.

I'd kissed plenty of guys, but none of them treated it like an act of worship. Tasting Ransom's tongue in my mouth was like experiencing the divine.

Maybe he was so pissy this morning because I'd pushed him to that point of no return? Or maybe the sex freak devil daddy actually *liked* kissing and cuddling? Maybe he was afraid I'd tell the other bunnies that inside his cool, polished exterior, was a scorching hot teddy bear with a giant cinnamon roll for a heart.

I felt a familiar warmth spreading through my core, and my breath quickened. If I could just hold onto this moment, I could handle any size or shape dildo thrown at me.

The music stopped, and I scrambled for the nearest chair. As I lowered myself onto the cock, I braced for the discomfort, but instead I found it much more bearable. It wasn't perfect, but it was better than nothing.

Round after round, I pushed through the aches and the lube and the humiliation, using my new strategy to make it more tolerable. I could feel my body adapting, learning to embrace the discomfort. But as the number of chairs dwindled, I knew my luck couldn't last forever.

"We're down to the last few chairs. Who will claim it?" Ransom announced, his voice a mixture of anticipation and amusement. The merman cock was back, shiny and wet, and this time bright green.

I wanted it.

I'd been waiting since round one.

When the music stopped, I lunged for the chair, but my body betrayed me—my legs were too weak, my timing too far off. I stumbled, grabbing the back of the chair, only for Dickface to shove me out of the way. I went flying onto the floor and watched as he skewered his ass down on the merman cock with a triumphant smirk.

That's when I noticed Ransom watching me. He shook his head in disappointment, then turned his attention back to the gamblers surrounding him. I watched him hand out one stack after another of gold chips. Not only had I lost this stupid game of musical chairs, but I'd made Ransom lose a lot of money.

Defeated, I could only lay there, bitter resentment coiling around my heart like a venomous snake. The laughter and catcalls from the crowd kept washing over me, and I felt the crushing weight of humiliation.

So the lesson for today was humility?

Man, I fucking *felt* it.

I felt anxiety rise up in me, the same awful feeling I had when my little sister Bianca gave me the heads up that I was being dragged online.

Unlike the fiasco with Remy and the shoe company using child labor in appalling sweatshops, I hadn't burst into tears and run away from this situation.

I had actually *tried* to do well at these Bunny Bondage Games.

I could've refused, could've sat in my cage all day and all night, could've gotten spanked or edged or dealt with whatever punishment Ransom gave me.

But I had fucking *tried*.

I'd tried so hard, pushed myself beyond my limits, only to humiliate myself in front of everyone in The Rabbit Hole. But beneath the shame, a tiny spark of defiance still flickered, refusing to be completely extinguished.

Maybe I didn't win this time, I thought, clenching my fists as I was escorted off the platform by one of the Tweedles. *But I'll show them all what I'm made of. No matter how many times they knock me down, I'll keep getting back up!*

"You did rather well tonight, bunny," Ransom whispered in my ear, his warm breath like soothing silk against my aching skin. I longed to pull open the zipper hiding my mouth, but I didn't dare defy my king in front of all these people. I was too busy trying to blink back tears of happiness.

I did *well?*

He was actually *praising* me?

He clipped my leash back onto my collar and I almost threw my arms around him. He gave me a stern look, gathering the slack into his hand. "Learn from your moment of defeat. Failing is what makes us stronger. It will make your eventual victory that much sweeter. Do you understand?"

I hesitated for a moment, then nodded firmly.

With cautious fingertips, he unzipped the mouth of my mask. I shuddered when his thumb ran along my lower lip. I hated him, yet I wanted him.

"Say it so I can hear you."

"I understand, my king. Failing is what makes us stronger."

"Good girl," he said with just a hint of affection in his tone.

It was all I needed.

All I wanted.

"These challenges aren't only about winning. They're about pushing your limits and growing stronger from each experience."

I looked into his eyes, feeling the ache of soreness melt into an ache of longing.

"But winning is what matters the most, right?" I gestured to the casino guests who were already spending the chips they'd won from him. "They're not here for personal growth. They're only here to win."

Ransom gave an offhand nod of acknowledgment.

"They can try as long as they like," he murmured in my ear. "But everyone knows that the house always wins."

CHAPTER
NINE

ALICE

"Say it so I can hear you . . . "

"Failing is what makes us stronger."

That mantra echoed in my mind as I continued to participate —and failed to win—in the Bunny Bondage Games. I kept coming in fourth, fifth, and sixth place. I was still in the running, but just barely. Every time I got pushed aside or knocked down, I got back up and wiped away the sweat from my face. Instead of wallowing in defeat, I let those words fuel me.

"Failing is what makes us stronger."

I needed to prove my worth, not only to Ransom but also to myself. I vowed to do whatever it took to become stronger, faster, and smarter.

Over the next handful of days, I pushed myself harder than ever before. I trained relentlessly, doing pushups in my cage, eating off the floor, and lifting weights until my arms trembled. If Ransom told me to do ten reps, I did fifteen. When mealtime came, I was already waiting in my designated place on my hands and knees.

I'd earned enough of my king's trust that he let me run laps

around the casino until my legs ached. I practiced yoga and medi-
tation, working on my flexibility and focus. No matter how
exhausted I became, I never allowed myself to quit.

"That's enough for now," Ransom would say, and I would
obey, gritting my teeth and pushing through the pain.

One evening, during a particularly grueling workout, Ransom
watched me closely, his eyes like a hawk's, searching for any sign
of weakness. As I completed my final set of push-ups, he nodded
approvingly.

"Good work, Alice," he said, his voice devoid of its usual
disapproval. "You're showing such dedication and determination.
This is exactly what I want to see from you."

My chest swelled with pride at his praise, and for the first
time since arriving in Wonderland, I felt a sense of accomplish-
ment. I was proving to Ransom—and to myself—that I could rise
above my failures and grow stronger from them.

"Thank you, my king," I panted, catching my breath. "I won't
let you down."

"See that you don't," he replied, his eyes glinting with something that might have been admiration. "If you continue to push
yourself like this, you just might become the champion Wonderland deserves."

And so, fueled by Ransom's rare approval and the burning
desire to prove myself to *me* instead of him, I continued to throw
myself into my training, my heart set on becoming the warrior
Wonderland needed.

No matter how tough the challenges ahead, I was ready to
face them head-on. Ransom might've thought I was a spoiled
brat, and Callister might've thought I was too old to be useful, but
I knew that beneath the blonde hair and big boobs lay a fierce,
unyielding spirit, just waiting to be unleashed.

Bring it on.

The soft click of my heels echoed through the dimly lit halls of
The Rabbit Hole as I followed Caramel through the labyrinth
with a newfound confidence. There was no competition tonight,
so we were allowed to relax and unwind.

Caramel had begged for permission to steal me away the
moment Ransom gave me unsupervised, off-leash privileges.

There were rules, though.

One: I wasn't allowed to tell them who I was. The refs called
me Blondie so that was my name now.

Two: I wasn't supposed to go anywhere alone.

Three: I had to keep my mask on at all times, just like all the
other bunnies.

Four: I had to wear clothes.

I'd been naked for so long that I'd stopped feeling self-
conscious about my body. Occasionally I'd admire my increased
muscle tone in the various mirrors of Ransom's room. My legs
looked amazing.

They looked even better now that I was in heels.

It felt familiar and foreign at the same time.

I almost preferred being barefoot, but I didn't dare tell my
king that I was unhappy with the outfit he'd given me.

The sultry garments Ransom had chosen clung to my body
like a second skin, revealing just as much as they concealed. The
black leather corset cinched my waist and accentuated my
curves, while the barely-there black lace panties left little to the
imagination. A black lace garter belt wrapped around my waist,
connecting the garter straps that held up my black stockings.

All the bunnies in The Rabbit Hole wore equally sexy outfits,
and Ransom was used to being surrounded by scantily-clad fuck
toys. But when I finished getting dressed and walked over to his
desk for inspection, whatever he was working on suddenly held

zero importance. An unrestrained flicker lit up his eyes in the softest, deepest shade of gold as he looked me up and down.

He liked what he saw.

Good.

He'd fucking *better*.

Still studying me, he leaned back in his chair, tenting his fingers while pursing his lips. Maybe he was thinking about revoking my privileges. Maybe he wanted his slutty little bunny to crawl across the floor and into his lap instead of going out to play with her new friend.

"If anyone in the club gives you trouble, you only need to say my name, and I'll deal with it."

"I thought I wasn't supposed to say your name, my king."

The look on his face told me this pleased him immensely.

"If you have to say my name, then I'll know it's for a good reason. Don't abuse this privilege, Alice."

"I won't. I promise, my king," I obediently replied. "I'll be back in time for dinner."

"See that you are," he said, and went back to his work.

Caramel was waiting for me as soon as I opened the door.

"Looking good, Blondie," she purred, her voice honey-sweet and dripping with seduction. She was a vision in her own right—long legs encased in fishnet stockings, soft waves of caramel-colored hair cascading down her back, and a tight black latex dress that hugged her every curve. Her matching black latex bunny mask obscured her face just enough to grant an air of mystery.

"Thanks," I replied, trying to sound nonchalant despite the heat rising to my cheeks. I was glad for my own bunny mask to hide my embarrassment as we went down to the casino. I couldn't deny the thrill of wearing such provocative clothes in front of so many people, but part of me still felt vulnerable under their gazes.

The guests knew better than to hound Ransom's bunnies for

insider tips on the next bondage game. It didn't stop them from sending us a free round of drinks. I don't know what the bartender handed us, but it was pink and delicious.

"Come on," Caramel beckoned after we finished our drinks. Her fingers grazed along my bare, un-cuffed wrist with tantalizing lightness. "There's so much more to see."

I hesitated, glancing over my shoulder for any sign of the Tweedles. Ransom hadn't granted me this level of freedom easily. I'd had to work really, really hard for it. Would he be okay with me poking around deeper into his dark, demonic domain?

On the other hand, the curious urge to find out where he'd hidden the Vorpal Sword tugged at me relentlessly. It was the same curiosity that led me to follow Winston, the White Rabbit, into Wonderland to begin with. I'd been living in this dream for so long that I felt like I belonged here.

It felt like home to me.

I bit back a laugh, recalling the mansion in Malibu that I'd traded for a cage that belonged to a mafia devil-daddy.

"I'll take that as a yes," said Caramel, her voice barely above a whisper. With that, she led me into the unknown.

As we ventured deeper into the heart of the club, the sultry atmosphere grew more intense. The sounds of moans and the scent of desire filled the air, mixing with the intoxicating allure of power that seemed to emanate from every corner.

I peered through a set of doors left ajar to see a woman bound with rope and hanging from chains attached to the ceiling, while another woman ate her pussy.

Another room was nothing but naked male bodies rolling around a cushioned floor, fucking and sucking and thrusting and coming like one giant living entity. My pussy clenched as I imagined diving into that pile of man meat and being devoured.

I couldn't help but be drawn into this world of darkness and pleasure, my senses heightened with each new sight and sound that I experienced.

"Enjoying yourself?" Caramel asked, her voice coy as she leaned in close, her breath warm against my ear.

"More than I thought I would," I admitted, surprised by my own honesty. This place, these people—they were unlike anything I'd ever known, and yet I found myself eager to explore it all.

"Good," she replied, a wicked smile playing on her lips. "That's the entire reason The Rabbit Hole exists."

As we continued our exploration, I couldn't shake the feeling that there was so much more to discover, not just about the sex club, but about myself as well. With Ransom as my guide and mentor, maybe I could unlock the secrets that lay hidden within me and actually find the strength to save Wonderland from the clutches of the Red Queen.

For now, though, I allowed myself to be swept up in the dark enchantment of the Rabbit Hole, ready to embrace whatever twisted fate awaited me.

Caramel led me further into the depths of the club, the dimly lit hallways casting eerie shadows on the walls. I couldn't help but shiver as we ventured deeper, the air thick with anticipation and the whispers of untold secrets.

"Stay close, Blondie," Caramel warned. "These halls can be quite ... disorienting."

She was right.

The black walls seemed to stretch into infinity, adorned only with flickering torches and more locked doors that piqued my curiosity. The maze-like pathways appeared indistinguishable from one another, making it all too easy to get lost in this labyrinth of pleasure and pain.

Caramel's face lit up when we found an unlocked door. She cautiously pulled it open, then hummed in delight as she stepped into the room.

"Ooohh, so *that's* where he put the merry-go-round. I've been wondering about that ... "

I pushed in past her, my brain struggling to register all the different things my eyes were seeing.

The room was filled with an array of BDSM equipment. There were St. Andrew's crosses and spanking benches, cages and suspension rigs—a perfect playground for those who craved both domination and submission.

A small gasp escaped my lips as I took in the sight, torn between fascination and trepidation.

"Where's the merry-go-round?" I asked, my voice barely a whisper as I clutched at the thin fabric of my outfit. My bunny mask, which shielded my true identity, felt like the only protection I had against the darkness that surrounded us.

"You'll see," Caramel replied cryptically, her caramel-colored hair swaying gently as she led me further into the room.

"Welcome to our playground," a woman announced behind me. I whirled around to see Trippy shutting the door and locking us all inside. "Took you long enough to get here."

My eyes widened in shock, and I glanced around to see half a dozen bunnies emerge from the shadows. I immediately recognized Dickface and the two male bunnies from the club doors . . . the same two bunnies who'd taken a swing at me after the pillow fight ended . . . and been immediately disqualified.

Trippy sidled up to me, her blue hair framing her nasty grin. "Sounds like you're interested in the merry-go-round. C'mon, boys! Let's show her how it works."

"She's probably already been on it," sneered a voice from beside me. I turned to see Dickface and the two other male sex slaves smirking at me. "Especially since she's the king's little pet."

"Back off, Dickface," I snapped, clenching my fists. It seemed my newfound status only made me a bigger target for resentment among the others.

"Enough with the naive little brat act," Trippy said, putting one hand on her hip. "We all know you're just sucking up to our king to get ahead in the Bunny Bondage Games," she accused, her eyes narrowing with disdain. The other two nodded in agreement.

"Sucking up?" I scoffed. "I've been working my ass off!"

Caramel stepped closer to me, her deep amber hair glinting in the dim torch light. "It's true, though," she chimed in. "You're getting special treatment from Ransom, and we all know it."

Dickface crossed his arms and huffed, "He hasn't fucked me since right after you showed up." His bitterness was palpable, and his words left me feeling exposed and vulnerable.

"Maybe you should learn how to fuck!" I retorted, trying to sound more confident than I felt.

"Or maybe," Dickface said with a wicked grin, "we should make sure our king doesn't find you attractive anymore."

I could feel the weight of their hungry eyes on me, eager for retaliation. I knew I needed to stand my ground, but I couldn't help the fear that tightened in my chest.

I turned to leave, but one of the door bunnies was standing in front of it.

"I don't think so, princess," he sneered, blocking my path. His muscular arms crossed over his broad chest, making it clear he wasn't going to let me pass without a fight.

"Get out of my way," I snapped, trying to keep my voice steady despite the fear that coiled in my stomach. My hands balled into fists at my sides, ready for anything he might throw at me.

"Aw," he taunted, stepping closer until our bodies were nearly touching. "What's the matter? Afraid to play rough?"

"Fuck off," I spat, my heart pounding. I tried to push past him, but his heavy arm shot out, pinning me against the cold, stone wall. The force of the impact left me breathless, my eyes widening in terror as I realized how vulnerable I truly was in that moment.

"Let's see if our king still wants you after we're done with you," he growled, his fingers digging painfully into my hips as he held me against the wall. Panic surged through me, my mind racing as I struggled to break free from his iron grip.

Before I could react, the two door bunnies had me pinned up against the wall. I tried to scream but Dickface clamped his hand over my mouth. The three of them pushed me down onto a small round padded platform at the center of the room.

My heart raced as I felt their hands holding me down. It didn't matter how hard I thrashed beneath them—they still managed to tie my wrists and ankles in place with rope.

My blood went ice cold as they attached the rope to metal bars strategically placed on the edges of the round platform. From under Dickface's calloused palm, I winced as I felt my arms and legs be pulled wide apart. More straps were fitted around my thighs, spreading me, binding me to the platform so that I couldn't move an inch.

Then Trippy joined in as they took turns ripping off the clothes from my body. Dickface tore off my mask and stuffed it in my mouth so I couldn't scream. Caramel had backed away from the other bunnies, her eyes wide as she watched her friends unleash their rage on me.

I lay there helplessly as they moved around me, their eyes gleaming with a cruel pleasure. They seemed to take delight in my terror as the male bunnies stood around me and slid their pants off to reveal their angry, eager cocks.

Fuck.

My tongue flailed around inside my mouth, trying to push the mask out, even though I knew exactly what was about to come next. Tears streamed down my face as I realized there was nothing I could do but accept whatever fate awaited me in this dark and twisted hellhole.

"Ready for a spin on the merry-go-round?" Trippy laughed. She grasped one of the metal bars and sent the platform spinning. The guys stepped forward just enough so that I got dick-slapped in the face over and over, faster and faster.

Harder and harder.

"This used to be the Red Queen's favorite game," Trippy said, spinning me faster. "Our king built mechanical cocks for her, but we like to play the old-fashioned way. Round and round and round it goes . . . where it stops, no one knows."

She grabbed onto the bar and dug her heels into the floor, bringing it to a jarring halt. My head was still spinning, but I came to my senses when I felt a pair of hands grasp my waist. Heat pushed between my legs, stinging as angry thrusts began jackhammering at my insides.

Tears streamed down my face as I tried to scream out for help but all that came out was muffled whimpering from behind the gag in my mouth. The bunny behind me started to thrust harder and faster.

Caramel looked on with wide eyes, yet anger was blazing in her voice as she shouted at the others to stop what they were doing to me.

Then Trippy spun the wheel again. Dicks slapped my wet cheek until I stopped spinning. I screamed into the leather as Dickface's monster cock loomed in front of my face.

"If you bite me, I'll fucking *kill* you," he warned from above. He pulled the mask out of my mouth and I sucked in a deep breath, not knowing if I'd have enough time to scream before he shoved his massive dick into my mouth.

"RANSOM!"

My scream was so loud it filled my ears.

It filled the entire room.

A gust of wind came out of nowhere, bringing along the scent of ozone and brimstone.

I remembered that smell.

Please . . . let it be him.

Let it be my king.

KING OF CLUBS

CHAPTER
TEN

RANSOM

Alice's scream pierced my skull like an arrow.

Panic flooded my thoughts through the window of her mind, the psychic bond between us alive with terror. I dropped my pen, papers scattering as I leapt from my chair.

The Tweedles standing outside my room startled as I threw open the door, magic crackling over my skin.

"Find Alice! *NOW!*"

Power surged through my veins as my body contorted and shifted. Bones cracked and reformed as I stormed down the hallway. Leathery wings burst from my back while horns spiraled out of my skull. I flexed my fists and rolled my shoulders, reveling in the rush of strength and magic.

Nothing could stand against me like this.

I threw my head back and roared, the walls of the casino floor shaking with the force of it. My heart pounded as I raced through my club, shoving gamblers and bunnies aside.

Alice let out another scream that reverberated through my mind. I closed my eyes and zeroed in on her location until I could see it in perfectly vivid detail. Dizziness swam through my head, magic propelling me forward in a burst of speed. Power surged and the world folded around me, spitting me out in a burst of brimstone and shadows.

I found myself in the storage room, the thick metal door bolted shut from the inside. A savage snarl tore from my throat at the nightmare scene that greeted me.

Alice was strapped face-down to the merry-go-round, her limbs splayed and tied, her clothes ripped to shreds. A handful of my bunnies surrounded her, jeering as one of them thrust into her mouth while another pounded into her from behind.

Grunts and the slap of flesh on flesh echoed off stone walls. The bunny between them waited his turn, his cock in hand. The blue-haired female capered around the men, giggling and egging them on as the second woman cowered in the corner, horror etched into her delicate features.

Rage exploded through me, dark and violent, searing away all reason.

I channeled all of it into my arms as my wings unfurled behind me. The bunny rutting into Alice was too lost in his plea-sure to notice the danger. I seized him by the ears of his mask and wrenched him back, his cock slipping free with a vulgar pop.

The other bunnies shrieked, scrambling away from Alice. I grabbed the male by the throat and lifted him into the air.

"You dare defile what belongs to me?" I squeezed, bone crunching under my demonic grip.

Dangling like a broken doll, he gurgled at the end of my arm, eyes bulging, clawing at my hand. His cock had gone limp, the cowardly bastard. I wanted to rip it from his body and stuff it down his throat.

I knew when to be patient.

But I also knew when to show no mercy.

Time to put this diseased bunny down for good.

I threw him across the room, where he hit the wall with a wet crack. A red smear of blood followed him as he slid to the floor in a crumpled heap. His neck was twisted at an unnatural angle, and his once handsome face was now misshapen from the force of his skull being smashed in. Brain matter squished from his eye sockets and through the holes in his mask.

Still raging, I glared at the other bunny who'd been waiting his turn to abuse Alice. Agony wracked his body as I began to systematically break each bone, my power keeping him alive and conscious so he could fully experience the pain. By the time I reached his legs he was little more than a mangled, sobbing wreck.

I growled in satisfaction as bone and sinew gave way beneath the force of my strength. I flung his corpse aside, letting him fall in a heap beside his dead companion.

Then I turned to the male who'd been raping Alice's mouth.

He'd been my favorite.

Not anymore.

"Forgive me, my king." He stumbled, tripping over his own feet before he dropped to his knees in front of me. But it was too late for apologies—the damage was done, and my instincts had taken over.

"Stand up and look at me."

He did as he was told. I crouched before him, baring my teeth. I grabbed his balls and squeezed until he let out a pathetic, mewling sound.

"If you want to fuck like an animal, then you can die like one."

I lowered my head and gored him with my horns through his abdomen, spilling intestines onto the floor. His shrieks rose to a fever pitch as I pinned him against the floor and tore off his limp cock. I shoved it into his throat, then dove back into his flesh, rending muscle from bone, using my fingers as claws.

His arms came away in a spray of bright red, and I kept punching at his ribcage with my fists, until chunks of his internal organs were splattered across the floor. When I finally felt he'd had enough, I stood up and looked down at his body.

It wasn't even a body.

It was a bloodstain ruining my closet floor.

I turned to the two women cowering in the corner just as the Tweedles unlocked the door and stepped into the room. They saw the pile of mutilated bodies, then shared a look, then waited for their orders.

My chest still heaving, I lifted a finger at the two females groveling on their hands and knees.

"Bind them and gag them, then put them in solitary confinement for now. I have yet to decide how to punish them."

"Very good, sir."

Silence fell as the Tweedles escorted the bunnies away. The emptiness was broken only by Alice's quiet sobs. I hurried to her side, magic slicing through her bonds with ease. A soothing rumble sounded in my chest as I scooped her into my arms. She curled into me, shaking and clutching at my bare chest.

"Shhh . . . You're safe now. I've got you."

She pressed her face into my neck, shoulders shaking with sobs. I cradled her close as her tears dampened my skin.

I never should have left her alone.

Never should've let her out of my sight.

"Nobody's going to hurt you ever again," I vowed, reaching up to cradle her cheek. She flinched at my feather-light caress but didn't pull away. It was progress, if small. I would earn back her trust, no matter how long it took.

She lifted her head, surprising me with her appearance. The wetness I'd felt wasn't her tears. It was the blood of her enemies, and she was bathed in it.

She'd never looked more fierce or beautiful to me than in that very moment.

My thumb traced the fullness of her lower lip, and I wondered if she had any idea of her destiny.

Alice peered past my shoulder at the wet puddles of mangled organs and crushed bone below my boots. Then she looked up at me, regarding me with a curious expression in her eyes.

It wasn't fear.

It was dark, savage joy.

Then she smiled, and I caught a glimpse of the warrior she would become.

"You're a monster," she whispered hoarsely.

Slowly, I nodded my head, accepting the condemnation with pride. "Yes, I am. But I'm *your* monster. I won't fail you again."

"You didn't fail me." Alice tilted her head up, meeting my gaze. Those blue eyes were clear and bright despite the horror she'd just faced. "You saved me."

I closed my eyes, holding her close and breathing in her scent —now tinged with the metallic bite of blood.

She was wrong. I hadn't saved her at all. If anything, she was the one saving me.

"You are far braver than you know." I brushed a kiss over her forehead, mindful of my horns. "And far more forgiving than I deserve."

"Oh, shut up," Alice sassed, her eyes meeting mine with determination. "You saved me, Ransom. You were there when I needed you. You came when I called. *That's* what matters. End of story."

I sighed heavily, my wings shifting as I tried to find solace in her words. But the gnawing feeling at the pit of my stomach persisted. It kept reminding me of the risk of danger that always seemed to follow Alice and the responsibility I'd taken on by hiding her . . . by training her . . .

By fucking her.

Now the girl was in my head.

But *how*?

Was it a sign that she was more to me than just a gorgeous little fuck toy? I gazed down at her, soaked in the blood of her enemies, and I immediately got hard at the sight of her wild, feral appearance.

She pulled back, her eyes searching my face. Then she leaned in. I growled, the sound inhuman and rough, and crushed my mouth to hers. She opened for me instantly, her tongue sliding against mine as she kissed me deeply. Her hands moved across my chest, caressing the rune tattoos that protected me as she tasted the blood on my lips.

Arousal stirred within me at her touch, intensifying as she broke the kiss and traced a line of kisses and bites down my neck. When she reached the juncture between my neck and shoulder, she sucked hard, marking me as hers.

The primal part of me purred in satisfaction at her claiming gesture.

My body caught fire at her touch, heat awakening despite the horrors surrounding us. I was immune to them. I fed on sex, not death. My only thoughts were of how fast I could get inside of her.

I shouldn't—not here, not now—but I was powerless to deny her.

I think she knew it.

"Where does it hurt?" I rasped, desire darkening my voice. "Tell me, and I'll kiss it better."

Alice looked up at me, her eyes gleaming. She tapped her neck, then brushed her fingers over the swell of her breast, before finally trailing her hand between her legs.

A growl rumbled in my chest as I my mouth curved into a wicked grin.

"Is that so?" I gently laid her on the bloody floor, pushing a half-crushed skull aside before crawling over her naked body. "Well then, it seems I have a lot of work to do."

My hands greedily explored her body as I continued my path lower, teasing her nipple with my tongue before closing my lips around it. I sucked hard, grazed my teeth over the hardened peak, then soothed it with a gentle swipe of my tongue.

Her fingers tightened in my hair, nails scraping against my scalp, and she ground her hips against me insistently. "Ransom, please ..."

"Begging already?" I chuckled, the sound dark and possessive. "Patience, bunny."

With deliberate slowness, I licked a trail of kisses down her stomach, dropping to my knees. The scent of her arousal, sharp and tangy, cut through the metallic stench of death clinging to us. I nuzzled her thigh, breathing in her scent before spreading her folds and leaning in for a taste.

Blood and viscera squelched beneath our bodies, but I paid no mind to the gore.

My focus was only on Alice.

I grazed my teeth over her clit, drawing a cry from her lips. "Where does it hurt?"

She grasped ahold of my horns, tilting my head up as she stared into my eyes. I saw the same mix of desire, trust and something far more dangerous reflected in her gaze.

Dominance.

"It hurts everywhere," Alice purred, rolling her hips again. "Kiss it better. Make me come."

I raised an eyebrow at her.

"Who decides when you come?"

She pressed her lips into a flat line. It wasn't a hard question. She knew the answer. She just didn't want to admit it.

But she surprised me by saying, "You do."

"Very good, Alice," I murmured, then sank into her velvet heat.

I lapped hungrily at her slick, pink core, erasing the trauma inflicted on her only moments ago. The taste of her sea-salt and arousal coated my tongue as I licked between her folds, parting the slit, and swirled around the hard little nub.

JEKKA WILDE

With every flick, a fiery passion ignited inside me and it burned brighter each time I teased her closer to the edge. Her moans grew louder and more desperate as she begged for release, while I relished in the satisfaction of giving her pleasure. I ravaged her sensitive clit with small circles that sent wave after wave of pleasure through her body.

Alice cried out, gripping my horns harder as her thighs trembled around my head. Her pleas grew more incoherent, her body shaking against me as she rode against my face, using me. She gasped, her hips twitching uncontrollably against me as I quickened my pace.

"The pain is gone," she panted, eyes glazed with desire. "I just want to come! Then I want you to fuck me!"

"Oh, I'm *definitely* going to fuck you," I replied with a wicked laugh.

I slid two fingers into her wetness, crooking them just so while sucking hard on her clit. Her hips lifted off the floor, pushing harder against my face.

She was almost there.

Such a good girl.

"Show me how hard you can come for me, Alice."

I pulled my slick fingers out, slid one of them into her ass, and thrust my tongue into her pussy. Her inner walls spasmed around me, gripping tight as she came with a howl.

She rocked her hips and grinded against my face, baptizing me with her juice as her hot, slippery cunt glided over my mouth and nose.

I pinned her wrists above her head as I stared down into her eyes. They were glazed with lust, pupils blown wide in the aftermath of her orgasm.

There was a heady rush of power in having her so vulnerable beneath me. I could do anything I wanted to her, take whatever I desired, and she would give it willingly.

"Ransom! Fuck me! I need you inside me *now*!"

"Not yet," I teased, crawling over her to cage her in with my arms. "I decide when to fuck you . . . and how to fuck you . . . "

A strangled cry escaped her. She bucked against me, writhing in a desperate bid for friction. I merely laughed and watched in amusement, savoring her torment.

"Please," she whimpered. All traces of defiance had fled her face, replaced by raw need. "Ransom, please . . . my king . . . "

Alice gazed up at me with eyes hazy from pleasure, a soft moan escaping her with every aftershock of ecstasy.

"Oh, you remembered your manners after all. That deserves a reward."

I snapped my fingers and made my boots and pants disappear. My length sprang forth, relieved to be free from restraint. Alice sighed in relief.

"You want it like this?" I rasped, grinding the thick head of my cock against her slick entrance. "Or do you want it like *this*?"

I rose up on my knees and let my secondary cock unwind from the primary shaft. Alice's eyes widened and her jaw fell open as she realized I could double her pleasure.

All she had to do was say the word.

My dual cocks throbbed, nearly painful in their ache to bury inside her body.

To claim what was mine.

To prove I could be the demon she needed.

"Want me to fill both your holes? Or do you want me to fuck your pussy until you can't walk?"

Alice whimpered, lifting up her hips in an offering to her king.

"Dealer's choice."

I lifted her waist and lined up my cocks to her wet pussy and her tight little ass. She gritted her teeth as I mounted her and slid into both of her holes inch by inch. I groaned at the feel of her tight heat swallowing me and stretching to accommodate my size. Her inner walls rippled around each cock, drawing me in deeper until the primary one bottomed out inside her.

When I'd buried myself to the hilt, I paused. I resisted the urge to thrust up into her tightness. Instead, I flexed both cocks simultaneously.

"Oh . . . fuuuuuuck . . . " she moaned.

We both shuddered at the sensation, a perfect completion that went bone deep. I waited until Alice rolled her hips, urging me to move.

Then I began to thrust.

Gentle.

Slow.

I let her get used to it.

Alice gasped into my mouth at the first few pumps, her slick channels yielding to my girth. I paused only a moment, waiting for her whimper of need before driving into her again and again.

Our harsh panting and the slap of flesh echoed off the walls. Alice rocked her hips to meet my punishing rhythm. Her nails caressed the base of my wings before raking down my back. The sting only fueled my arousal, my thrusts turning savage as I claimed what was mine.

Her inner walls fluttered and clenched, pulling me in deeper. The coil of heat in my gut threatened to snap—but not yet. Not until she came apart around my cocks.

I began to ride her even harder, watching her breasts bouncing with every thrust as she surrendered her pleasure to me. I watched through half-lidded eyes, utterly entranced by the sight of her getting fucked among the twisted bodies and the slurry of crushed bones and blood. She was surrounded by death, yet so warm and alive, so close to the brink of coming apart beneath me.

She spread her legs wider, taking both my cocks in one smooth glide after another. I groaned at the sensation of having more room to fill.

"Does my slutty little bunny like getting fucked by her monster?"

"Yeah," she whimpered.

"You'll take whatever I give you, and you'll be grateful for it, won't you?"

"Fuck yeah," she shuddered with a breathy moan.

"I love how you're taking both my cocks right now," I told her, thrusting harder. "I wish you could see what I see . . . they're all wet and shiny from your dripping wet pussy. Both my cocks are stretching you out so wide. I love that you let me fuck you this way."

"Will you fuck me like this in your room?" she asked. "I wanna see my reflection in your mirrors. I wanna watch you fuck me with both demon cocks."

I immediately pulled out of her—the only thing stopping me from blowing my loads right then and there was the sensation of cool air on my wet shafts.

"You bad little bunny," I scolded through my teeth. "You almost made me come."

I backed up and burrowed my face into her cunt one more time, sucking her clit and massaging with my tongue. Alice cried out beneath me, her nails grabbing my horns one more time, but I pushed them away just as she drew near the edge of release.

Time to push her over to the other side.

I grabbed her by her bloody hips and skewered both holes with my rock-hard shafts, then pounded mercilessly into her. The slap of sweaty flesh echoed through the room, underscored by our ragged moans. The sounds spurred me on, making my hips slam deeper . . . harder . . . faster.

"I need to come," she pleaded, cheeks flushed. "Please, I'm so close . . ."

"Not yet." I began to move again, a slow, relentless grind that had her gasping anew. "You will come when I allow it, and not before." I bent to nip at her throat, my fingers digging into her hips to hold her in place. "Understand?"

"Y—yes," she moaned. "I understand, just please . . . "

"Please what?" I hissed against her skin. "Tell me what you want, Alice."

"I want to come," she cried. "And I want you to come inside me!"

"Tell me why you want my cum inside you." I pulled out slowly, then drove back in with enough force to wring a cry from her throat. Her slick heat gripped me like a vise as I pounded into her, chasing the peak of pleasure for us both.

"It's so warm," she panted. "It's so hot I can feel it . . . and I love knowing how deep inside my body you are."

Fucking hell.

I was so fucking close to losing it. All I had to do was make her go first, and I'd follow right after her.

"I like knowing that, too. I'm going to come inside your pussy . . . *and* your ass. And I'm going to do it at the same time."

I could feel her stomach clench with anticipation, her inner walls rippling in the telltale sign she was about to fall into oblivion. I shifted, sliding almost completely out of her before slamming back in.

The new angle had the head of my main cock stroking over her g-spot with every thrust. Without asking, she pinned her gaze on mine, fighting her climax until I gave her permission to let go.

"That's my good girl." I slid a hand between us, fingers circling the swollen nub of her clit. "Keep your eyes on me. Now come for me, Alice."

She screamed and arched her back off the floor as euphoria ravaged every nerve and every cell in her body. Her pussy's inner walls clamped down, rippling with such powerful contractions and spasms along my length that I felt them in my balls. Her asshole squeezed down on my second cock until the stimulation was too much for me to bear.

Her climax hit her like a storm, one broken wail after another tearing from her lips. The coil of tension in my gut tightened impossibly as her orgasm triggered my own. Heat and pressure built up at the base of my spine as her body clenched around me.

With a low, deep groan, I unleashed my seed inside her. Hot spurts of cum flooded from my twin cocks into both of her channels until it leaked out around where our bodies were joined. Her cunt and her asshole squeezed around my length, milking me for all that I had.

A cry of pleasure burst from her lips, nails digging into my back, holding onto me for dear life.

Although my rhythm turned erratic, I kept fucking and thrusting, riding every final wave of my orgasm until I'd completely emptied my balls into her.

"Yes . . . " Alice moaned as I collapsed half on top of her, still buried inside the warmth of her body. "Give it all to me."

She wrapped her arms around me, holding me close as we came down from the high. No other words were needed in this moment. Our connection went beyond such things.

I held her close as our breathing slowed, my softening cocks still nestled inside her warmth. I kept one hand tangled in her messy, bloody hair while resting my weight on my elbow.

Her fingers traced lazy patterns over my back while her nails scratched lightly between my wings.

It felt divine.

So utterly divine.

"You know . . . if you're not careful, you're gonna get me addicted to this." Her words were muffled against my chest.

I chuckled, the sound rumbling in my chest. "You already are, little bunny."

Alice tilted her head up, eyes gleaming. "Maybe I am."

A surge of warmth flooded me at her words. Mindful of my horns, I leaned down, capturing her lips in a slow, deep kiss.

A loud bang at the door had us jerking apart.

"Boss!" One of the Tweedles' panicked voices came through the door. "We got a situation upstairs!"

I growled, reluctantly withdrawing from Alice's warmth to stand. What was so fucking important that the Tweedles felt they had to interrupt us?

Another bang rattled the door on its hinges. "Boss, it's seriouser and seriouser!"

Every muscle in my body tensed as I stepped over broken bodies and organs and flung open the door. Tweedle Dee and Tweedle Dum had worked for me long enough that they didn't flinch at the sight of me naked, covered in blood, and clearly displeased.

"Explain. Now." My voice was deceptively calm, though anger simmered beneath.

Tweedle Dee took a step forward, lowering his voice. "The Red Queen knows Alice is here. Her army is marching on The Rabbit Hole as we speak. She'll be here in a matter of hours!"

I clenched my jaw in outrage.

I ran a tight ship. All my staff were fully vetted. Who the *fuck* had betrayed me?

"How did you learn this information?" I asked.

"Chess and Hatter just arrived with Callister," said Tweedle Dee. "The Queen had them all imprisoned, but they escaped. Nobody else knows they're here. I told them you'd want to speak to them immediately."

"You're right," I said, tamping down the warring emotions filling my brain. I turned to Alice and frowned. "We'll be there at once."

CHAPTER
ELEVEN

ALICE

With a wave of his hand, Ransom's demon magic made the mutilated bodies in the storage room vanish into thin air. The blood evaporated off the floor, and the shredded remains of my clothes were replaced with a simple, elegant black dress.

My heart pounded as the King of Clubs shifted back into his human form, in yet another impeccable black suit. His wings and horns faded away like a dream.

What the fuck had just happened?

One minute I was face down on the merry-go-round, being assaulted by a couple of motherfuckers. The next, Ransom erupted into a nightmarish beast, annihilating the bodies of my attackers.

Then he'd fucked me into oblivion on a bed of their corpses.

And the most fucked up thing of all?

I *liked* it.

A *lot*.

No . . . I take that back.

I fucking *loved* knowing the extent of just how far Ransom's brutal, unhinged passion could go when it came to protecting me.

159

I could feel it in the lingering ache in my core, the slippery heat that he'd left behind, the proof of his affection that was now slowly trickling down my thighs . . . reminding me just how little self-control he had when it came to me.

In a possessive move that turned me on all over again, Ransom ordered the Tweedles to find out the Red Queen's ETA. Then he took my arm and pulled me close. He led me down the hall until we found the nearest elevator and went straight to his room.

Granted, we hadn't known each other that long, but I'd never seen him like this before.

Was he furious?

Sure.

Aroused?

In a way, I guess . . .

No, this was peak mafia devil-daddy realness, and his focus was strictly on dealing with shit that needed to be done.

He paced back and forth on the black and gold tile floors, distracted by his thoughts.

Suddenly he stopped and stared directly at me.

"Fuck. I never asked if you were alright." He curled his hand into a fist, his gold pinky ring catching on the light. "*Are* you alright?"

I blinked, not knowing how to respond.

"Uhhh . . . can I get back to you on that? I need some time to process everything."

"There's no time," he said sharply, walking over to me. "What do you want? What do you need? A blanket? Tea? Wine?"

I studied his face carefully, amazed that murdering my attackers with his bare hands didn't seem like enough to him.

"I wouldn't mind a long, hot shower, but I suppose there's no time for that, either."

Ransom shook his head, his expression severe.

I gave a hopeless shrug.

"Wine's good . . . although . . . "

"Although . . . ?"

I felt my face heat up with a blush of embarrassment, and I didn't understand why. Why should I feel embarrassed when Ransom had fucked me with a giant strawberry? He'd made me squirt all over him until I ruined his suit. He'd fucked me in a pool of blood. He'd stuffed my ass with whimsy whirls, yet somehow, I felt too embarrassed to tell him what I wanted right now?

Why?

Was it too vanilla? Too immature? Too innocent?

"Use your words, Alice. I can't read your mind like Chess can."

I looked down at the floor, struggling to find my voice.

Just say it, I thought. *Just make the sounds with your mouth hole and get it out there. However he reacts will say more about him than it will about you. You got this.*

I took a deep breath, then looked straight into his dark, brooding eyes. "I could really use a hug."

He tilted his head to one side, studying me as if I'd asked my question in pig Latin.

"You want me to . . . *hold* you?"

"Yeah," I nodded, feeling more confident about my request. "That was some pretty intense shit that just happened."

"Things are about to become more intense," he replied, but it didn't stop him from closing the distance between us and gathering me into his arms.

Warmth wrapped around me like a cocoon as he pressed me into his hard chest, shielding me from harm. The same hands that were capable of breaking bones and crushing skulls were now caressing my body with tender care. I melted into him, letting my weight sink against his inhuman strength.

Letting out a soft sigh of resignation, he lifted my chin, then reached for my throat. I yielded to him without thinking, not knowing what was about to happen, yet trusting him completely.

To my surprise, he unfastened the collar around my neck. Shock rippled through me as Ransom stripped away the symbol of my imprisonment. I was no longer just his plaything, hidden behind a mask, dominated by my collar.

I'd become something more.

I took a deep breath and let it out, feeling a deep, raw pang of emotion when his hand caressed my hair. With every stroke I was made clean, feeling like I'd just stepped out of a warm bath. My skin tingled with softness and my hair became soft and silky. My mind felt like it had been fortified against the traumatic memories of what I'd seen . . . of what I'd experienced. He didn't take my memories away, but he took away the pain.

I looked up at him in wonder. "How did you do that?"

He lifted a brow at me. "Do what?"

"You took my pain away."

Ransom shook his head, then held up my collar. It disappeared in a puff of sparkling smoke, surrounding us with twinkles of magic. He brought his hand to my cheek, cradling my face, gazing down at me with bittersweet pride.

"I didn't make your pain go away, Alice. *You* did."

My fingers inspected my bare throat as I continued to stare at him in disbelief.

"You mean . . . my imagination's back?"

He nodded slowly.

"Yes. You wanted something so much that you made it real. Imagine that glass of wine you want. See what happens."

I took a step back and visualized a tall stem of Cristal. One instantly appeared in front of me, hovering in the air.

"Are you *serious* right now?" I squealed as I took the champagne into my hand. It looked like Cristal. It smelled like Cristal. I brought it to my lips and tipped my head back.

It sure tasted like Cristal.

"Try not to drink any more than that," he said with a cautious smile. "I'm going to need you alert and ready for anything."

The air inside the room suddenly shifted, and I wondered if lightning was about to strike.

As if on cue, Chess and Hatter burst through the door holding up Callister between them. Their faces were fraught with exhaustion and tension. I set down my wine and made a beeline for them.

"Callister!" I gasped, my voice laced with shock as I took in his haggard appearance.

His clothes were torn to shreds and stained with violet blood. His teal pompadour was flattened against one side of his face, stuck there with blood and sweat. Deep gashes covered his body, and bruises bloomed across his skin like grotesque flowers. His lip was split and one eye was swollen shut. Seeing him so horribly broken made my stomach turn.

"What happened?" Ransom's voice was deceptively calm, but rage simmered beneath the surface.

"The Queen is coming!" Hatter exclaimed, his mismatched eyes wide and darting around the room. He slammed the door shut and bolted the locks.

Ransom palmed his face and shook his head.

"I'm well aware of the situation, Hatter. I meant, what happened to Callister?"

"Roxanne did a number on him," said Chess while easing Callister onto one of the two velvet sofas.

Ransom cursed under his breath, turning away to conjure himself a drink. The glass shattered in his grip, the shards turning into a glittering cloud of gold as his rage intensified.

Fury bubbled up inside of me as well.

"Who the fuck is Roxanne?" I demanded.

"The Red Queen," Callister winced, clutching his ribs as he gingerly repositioned himself on the sofa. Ransom came over, standing across from him, his arms folded across his chest in anger. "I didn't tell her anything, Ransom. She doesn't know we're here, but she knows Alice is."

163

"She doesn't know that for a fact," Chess clarified as he turned to Ransom. "What she *does* know is that Alice was seen with Callister. There must've been a spy at Hatter's tea party. And she knows Callister was with you quite recently." He tossed a small gold object over to Ransom, who caught it in midair. He held it out and studied it, then frowned.

My heart nearly stopped as I realized what he was holding.

It was a gold chip from The Rabbit Hole casino.

The same kind of chip used for the card game he and Callister had been playing when I first arrived here. I remembered they'd been playing with stacks of those chips.

Ransom's eyes squeezed shut, his jaw clenching. When he finally met my gaze, there was so much unspoken regret in his eyes.

Nobody had betrayed him, after all.

It was a mistake. A terrible, horrible, stupid mistake.

And poor Callister had paid the price.

My heart clenched at the sight of the teal-haired caterpillar, so battered and broken in comparison to the Cheshire Cat sitting next to him. Although our relationship had been rocky at best, I couldn't help but feel sympathy for Callister.

I stepped past Chess and sat down beside his friend—our friend—and imagined a first aid kit and a bowl of warm, soapy water, and a stack of clean washcloths. They appeared on a small table next to me.

"Let me help you," I murmured as I soaked one of the cloths in the clean water. I wrung it out and carefully dabbed it against the violet blood covering Callister's face. He flinched slightly but didn't pull away.

"Would you like a hand with that?" Chess asked, taking off his jacket and rolling up his sleeves. "I can stitch him up. I'm rather good with string."

"Sure." It was impossible not to grin at the thought of the enigmatic and sensual Cheshire Cat batting at a piece of string.

164

He caught my gaze with his hypnotic green eyes and I knew he was searching my thoughts, making sure I was okay.

I gave him a soft smile and nodded.

Given the circumstances, I was doing alright.

"I'm so sorry," I said to Callister as I continued to wash away the blood and grime coating his skin. Guilt gnawed at my insides whenever he winced, every movement I made clearly agony for him. "This was my fault. If I hadn't come to Wonderland in the first place . . . if I hadn't needed your help finding the Vorpal Sword . . . none of this would've happened."

Callister cracked his good eye open and peered down at me.

"You're not the one who beat the ever-loving-shit out of me. You're not the one who killed my brother over a *rose*. You're not the one who's singlehandedly destroying Wonderland."

The more blood I washed away, the more clearly I saw just how deep some of Callister's wounds went. I switched places with Chess to let him stitch the deeper cuts. My stomach turned at the sight as I imagined the torture he must have endured. I swallowed hard, fighting back tears.

Now wasn't the time.

Besides . . .

Tears weren't going to help anyone.

"Maybe it's not my fault directly," I told him as I ripped open a box of butterfly bandages, "but it doesn't stop me from feeling sorry that this happened to you."

A ghost of a smile touched his lips. "I'll heal. And besides . . . " His gaze softened. "You're worth it."

My cheeks heated at his words. I busied myself with bandaging a gash on his arm, unsure of how to respond. I didn't want to read too much into a few kind words.

For all I knew, he was concussed.

He winced again, and I realized I was going to need a better way to distract him while I finished my work.

Closing my eyes, I put my imagination to work and thought of the best way I knew how to distract Callister.

A blow job?

I heard Chess laugh under his breath at hearing my thoughts.

Fuck! That's not what I meant!

"I'm sure he wouldn't mind," Chess murmured as he stitched up a gash on Callister's tattooed shoulder.

I held back a sheepish grin, then tried again.

"Here," I said, handing Callister a lit cigarette. "It's my favorite flavor."

"Curiouser and curiouser," he hummed. Cautiously, he took it from me, his fingers brushing against mine before he brought it to the side of his split lip. With his one good eye still peering at me, he took a long drag. The tobacco crackled before filling the space around us with a sweet, spicy smell that immediately put me at ease.

"What flavor *is* this?" he asked. White smoke curled and rolled off his tongue before being sucked back into his mouth.

Chess paused in between stitches and lifted his nose to the air, his brow furrowing as he tried to figure it out.

"I smell whipped cream and cinnamon . . . and a dash of nutmeg, but there's something else underneath. Is it cake?"

"No."

"I smell coffee," Hatter said, taking off his hat and plopping down on the sofa across from us. "Is it coffee, or am I mad?"

"You're mad," Chess told him.

"But he's not wrong," I grinned. "It's a pumpkin spice latte. Best thing ever."

"Damn near perfect," Callister agreed with a nod. His body began to relax and Chess and I were able to finish treating his injuries by the time he finished his PSL cigarette.

"Not too bad, Nurse Alice," he said, admiring my work. "Looks like I'll live to vex you another day."

"We might not have another day," Ransom said, concern

etching his features. He came over to join us, although he didn't sit down. His fingers grasped the back of the sofa as he leaned forward. He looked like he was trying to decide whether to break it in half or throw it across the room. "We need a plan. And quickly. The Red Queen will be here with her soldiers sooner than we think. What's it going to be? Fight or flight?"

"The Red Queen doesn't know for certain that we're here," said Chess, trying to remain calm. "She doesn't even know for sure that Alice is here. What if we take Alice and the Vorpal Sword and go straight to the White Queen's court?"

"It won't stop her from killing the guests of The Rabbit Hole in search of her," said Ransom. "You know how murderous she gets when she's angry."

"Are you suggesting we fight?" Chess replied. "With what army? Are you going to arm your bunnies with dildos and beat the queen's soldiers to death?"

I muffled a laugh at the thought.

"You could hide Alice in Hell," Hatter suggested. "Roxanne's human. She can't go there."

"She can go there, she just can't come back," Chess told him. "It would be the same with Alice. Humans can't come back if we took them to Hell."

"Why not?" I asked.

"Your soul prevents it," said Chess. "Going to hell is a one-way trip for anyone with a soul. Since demons don't have souls, we can come and go as we please."

"Got it. I definitely don't want to go to Hell. Not even for a little bit."

"Then we hide Alice somewhere else," Callister said. "You could use the Looking Glass to send her back to her world. The Queen can't follow her there."

Hatter perked up at this idea.

"Ah, yes! And without Alice, she has no reason to destroy Wonderland."

"She's already destroying it!" Ransom snapped. "Whether or not Alice is here, Roxanne won't be satisfied until our world is nothing but ashes and despair. Sending Alice away only delays the inevitable."

"I'm not hiding anywhere," I said, crossing my arms defiantly over my chest. I wasn't about to run away like a coward, leaving Wonderland at the mercy of that monster. These wicked boys had become my friends—even Callister. I couldn't abandon them now, when it mattered the most. "There's *got* to be another way."

"If we don't run, then we fight," Callister growled. "Teach the bitch a lesson once and for all."

"With what army?" Ransom snapped in thinly veiled exasperation. "In case you haven't noticed, you're next to useless right now and Hatter's going mad before our very eyes! Roxanne has us outnumbered. A direct attack would be suicide."

"We could create a spectacular diversion," Hatter chimed in, still lying across the other sofa. "Let's throw a masquerade ball! Everyone loves a party. The Queen will be so busy drinking and dancing that she won't even remember why she came here."

Ransom peered down his nose at the fae sprawled out below him. He looked like he wanted to strangle him. "Do you even *hear* yourself, you fuckwit? This isn't a game!"

"This fuckwit may have a point," Chess mused, actually considering the suggestion. "Roxanne's vanity is her weakness. If we give the appearance of a grand spectacle, she may lower her guard. And if we're all in disguise, she won't know who is who. We could hide in plain sight."

"It could work." Hope flickered inside me. "If she thinks she's walked into a huge party, she won't be expecting an attack."

Callister was silent, gazing into the shadows, his eyes distant. Finally, he looked at me, a strange light entering his eyes. "Actually . . . " he said softly, "this might be the perfect opportunity for us to kill the Red Queen. We could use Alice as bait to lure her in, then ambush her. Take her out. Problem solved. Then we can be rid of her forever."

Ransom's eyes flashed with anger.

"Absolutely not! If you ever suggest using Alice as bait again, I will rip out your entrails and strangle you with them! Are we clear?"

"Ransom, he's right," I said, gentle but firm. "It could work. I can distract the Red Queen long enough for you guys to kill her."

"You don't understand," he said with a grim expression. "Whether it's the Red Queen or her Jabberwocky, *you're* the one who has to deliver the death blow. We can't do it. It has to be you."

"Oh . . . " I whispered, shrinking under their gazes.

"I won't put you in harm's way."

"She's already in harm's way," Callister said from beside me. "If we want to end this, Alice needs to face the Red Queen."

"She's not ready. It's too dangerous," Ransom argued, but Callister was already shaking his head. With a significant amount of effort he rose from the sofa and pulled himself to his feet. He straightened, meeting Ransom's gaze.

"Will she ever be ready enough?" he asked through bared teeth. "You see what the Red Queen has done to me! You know what she's done to my brother, to our friends, to everyone we've ever known. If we want to defeat her once and for all, we need Alice. This would be the perfect opportunity, and you fucking know it!"

"We can handle Roxanne, if you're willing to finish her off," Chess said to me. "You have the Vorpal Sword. Use it to end Roxanne's reign of terror over Wonderland once and for all."

A surge of determination rose inside me. I swallowed hard, my heart pounding. Could I really face the Red Queen? What if I wasn't strong enough to finish the job?

Callister put his hand on my shoulder, as if sensing my fear. "You won't face her alone. We'll be right there with you." His eyes gleamed. "Time to show Roxanne she fucked with the wrong Alice."

My chest tightened. I knew the Red Queen would stop at nothing to get what she wanted—my head.

"Even if you guys helped me, I don't have the sword," I admitted before glancing at Ransom.

"Where is it?" Callister asked.

"It's not here," said Ransom. "I put it somewhere safe."

"Where?"

"Somewhere the queen will never find it. That's all you need to know."

"You took it to Hell, didn't you?" Callister scoffed.

Ransom clenched his jaw, irritation flickering in his eyes at the accusation. "I have it under control," he growled. "This isn't up for discussion."

"We're discussing it right *now*!" Callister argued. "You'd better go get it!"

Ransom's eyes narrowed at his friend but said nothing.

Chess leaned against the back of the sofa, arms crossed, gaze thoughtful. "While I don't doubt your judgment, Ransom, the Vorpal Sword is our only hope of defeating Roxanne. Leaving it in Hell could prove problematic. This could be our only chance to get rid of the Red Queen forever. Please . . . I know it's not how things have always been done, but think of the greater good."

Ransom's jaw tightened, a muscle twitching. I bit my lip, staying silent. This wasn't my place to intervene, but I agreed with Callister and Chess.

After a brief, yet tense moment, he sighed.

"Fine." He ran a hand through his dark hair, frustration etched into his handsome features. "But you'll have to be the one to fetch it. I have to prepare my club and my staff for the queen's arrival."

Chess studied Ransom, his green-eyed gaze inscrutable. "Of course I'll go to Hell. Just tell me where to look."

As Ransom gave a description of landmarks, I felt a fiery surge of warmth and affection for these men who were willing to go to Hell and back to save their world. No matter the danger ahead, as long as I had them by my side, I knew I could face anything.

Even the Red Queen.

CHAPTER
TWELVE
ALICE

I watched as Chess faded into the air, particle by particle. Callister swayed unsteadily on his feet, and I leapt up to help him sit back down on the sofa with me. His violet blood seeped through the dressings covering his body, creating an unsettling contrast against the white gauze.

"Oh no! You're bleeding through your bandages!"

Callister grimaced, his eyes glassy with pain. I could tell he was trying to suppress the anguish that radiated through his body. His tattoos of insects and snakes seemed to writhe in pain, mirroring their owner's agony.

"His wounds are deeper than I realized," Ransom observed, his voice laced with concern.

"The raven queen dances under the midnight sky," Hatter babbled from the sofa across from me, "while Callister the Caterpillar shifts between the shadows." He paused, blinking at me with a hint of recognition. "Alice? Is that you?"

"Yeah, it's me," I assured him, although worry was starting to gnaw at my insides. Hatter's deteriorating mental state was almost as concerning as Callister's injuries. I tried to imagine

Hatter returning to sanity and Callister's pain to stop, but it didn't work.

Desperate, I looked to Ransom for help. "They're getting worse. Why aren't they getting better?"

"There's too much dark energy around them. It's blocking their magic."

I threw my hands up in frustration.

"Great. So how do we help them? Is there anything we can do?"

"There's a way . . . " he began, his eyes darkening. "The energy blocking their magic has to be pushed out of the way by even stronger energy."

"Like what?"

Ransom's eyes flicked over to Callister.

"No," he said, frowning so hard that his split lip started bleeding again.

"Just tell me what to do, and I'll do it!" I insisted. The tension in the room was palpable, setting my nerves on edge.

But when Ransom slid me a heated look, warmth began to pool low in my belly.

I knew what that look meant.

"To heal Callister and restore Hatter's mind, we'll need an . . . unconventional method. One that harnesses and focuses our combined magical energies."

My cheeks flushed as understanding dawned on me. "You can't mean—"

I looked at Callister to see a wry smile curving his bloody lips. "You'd have to make us come. Right here. Right now. And given that we don't have much time, and you don't know the first thing about how I like to fuck, I don't think you'd be able to do it."

I froze. "You can't be serious."

"He's right. Sexual energy is the most powerful magic there is." Ransom shrugged. "But the choice is yours."

"Can't you guys just jerk off and be done with it?"

"It would be exponentially faster if you helped them along," said Ransom. "You're *much* more enticing than an empty hand."

"Callister doesn't even *like* me!"

"That doesn't mean I wouldn't still destroy your cunt if given the chance," he coolly replied.

I gaped at them, torn between shock and curiosity. On one hand, the suggestion was outrageous. But if it could honestly get my wicked boys back in working order . . .

I bit my lip, aware of Ransom and Callister and even Hatter watching me with predatory intensity. My hesitation wavered in the face of this challenge—along with my desire.

"What have I told you about biting your lip?" Ransom asked. He stepped close to me and reached out, tilting my chin up to meet his gaze. His touch sent sparks dancing across my skin.

"That it's your job . . . my king."

Ransom's smile was slow and wicked, sending delicious anticipation unfurling inside me. He cupped the back of my neck, leaned down, then pulled me into a scorching kiss right in front of Callister. As our tongues entwined, magic ignited—and I gave myself over to the madness of Wonderland.

"How badly do you want to help your king? Your friends?" His voice was a silken caress, tempting and irresistible. "This isn't the only way . . . but it's the most efficient."

Heat rushed through me as I made my decision. I imagined myself naked, and suddenly I was. I lifted my chin and met his eyes.

"Hatter," I said while staring directly at Ransom. "Come over here and fuck me."

"Is it alright if I wear my hat? I fuck better with my hat on."

"Then you'd better put it on."

I turned around and knelt on the couch cushions, draping my arms over the back, bringing myself face-level with Ransom's crotch. Instead of giving me his cock, he pulled up a chair to watch.

Hatter slid behind me, his hands skimming down my sides to grip my hips. His lips brushed the nape of my neck, his teeth nipping playfully. "Oh Alice . . . such a sweet, thoughtful girl . . ." His praise sent a throb of heat between my legs.

Ransom leaned forward, and I moaned into his mouth as Hatter ground against me, the hard length of his cock pressing into the back of my thigh. My hands tangled in Ransom's hair, kissing him desperately.

A harsh cough interrupted us. We broke apart to find Callister watching us, a scowl twisting his bloody lips. But the impressive bulge straining against his pants revealed his irritation.

"Forgetting someone?" he demanded, his words dripping with sarcasm despite his weakened state. His hungry gaze lingered on me in a way that made me ache.

"Tell her what you want," said Ransom.

Meanwhile, Hatter's hands slid between my thighs, his fingers spreading my wet lips apart. I arched my back and lifted my ass higher, fully exposed to his appreciative stares. Then his hands gripped my hips, and with one hard thrust he buried himself inside my pussy.

A guttural groan rumbled in Callister's chest as he watched me get penetrated.

"I want my friends to treat your gash like a fucking cum dumpster while you suck me off," he said with a twisted smirk. "And after they're done, I want to dive into it and trash it some more. But I don't think you've got the stomach for it."

Even though I was getting plowed by Hatter, I glared at him. "You don't think I can handle you guys running a train on me? I've already fucked two of you. Three if you count Chess."

Callister let out a contemptuous laugh. "I don't think you can handle *this*."

He unfastened his belt with a metallic rasp and pulled his torn pants down his injured legs, freeing his cock.

It was unlike anything I'd seen before.

Deeply ridged and glistening, it looked like it belonged to an insect. The tip was such a dark shade of teal that it almost looked black, then it faded the closer it got to his body. The shaft was narrower at the base and got thick and fat in the middle, then tapered into a soft point at the end. Short spikes covered the bulge at the base, making me wonder how the fuck this guy got laid.

No wonder he was always in such a bad mood.

Fear and fascination battled it out in my mind at the sight of his metamorphic dick. Ransom chuckled, bending to lick the shell of my ear. "Our Callister is full of surprises. But don't worry, Alice—his venom will only increase your pleasure."

I swallowed hard, torn between apprehension and curiosity. But one look at Callister's smug expression had me convinced. I would never give him the satisfaction of seeing me back down from this challenge.

Steeling myself, I wrapped my fingers around the strange organ. It was hot to the touch, pulsing with life, and squishier than I was expecting. A sound like an angry hiss escaped Callister's lips.

"Are you going to suck it or not?"

"Shut up, or I'll use my teeth," I snapped, giving him a tight warning squeeze that was meant to hurt. Instead, Callister groaned in pleasure.

"Go on and use them," he taunted, pushing his hips towards my hand. "I can handle the pain."

"We'll see." I kept squeezing hard, jerking him off while Ransom stood up and pressed his cock against my cheek. I shot Callister a seductive smile, then opened wide and took Ransom into my mouth.

The fat insect cock in my hand swelled even thicker as I stroked up and down. The ridges became more pronounced, and the spikes at the base got bigger. I let my palm bounce off of them a few times and discovered they were surprisingly soft. Maybe fucking this freak wouldn't be that bad.

Hell . . . I might even like it.

I lost myself in the rhythm of sucking Ransom's cock and tugging on Callister's shaft that I was barely aware of Hatter pulling out of me and positioning the head of his dick against my asshole.

A cry escaped me at the sensation of him plunging deep into my ass. The feeling of being filled so completely from both ends was nearly overwhelming. My left hand tightened on Callister's ridged length, stroking in time with Hatter's thrusts. My right hand had found my clit and began to massage in small, slow circles.

Hatter set a brutal pace, hips snapping against my ass as he fucked me. Each thrust drove Ransom's cock deeper into my throat.

He caught my chin again, forcing me to meet his gaze. Warm glints of gold shone in his eyes, gleaming with dark promise. "Look at me, Alice. Look at me while my friends and I fuck you."

I whimpered but obeyed, trapped by the command in his voice and the cocks pistoning inside my ass and my mouth. The pain and pleasure mingled into something exquisite, heat coiling tight in my belly. I was so close, teetering on the edge as they pounded into me.

I rubbed my clit harder . . . faster.

Fuck . . . Callister's cock was so fat and squishy and textured.

I was *definitely* going to fuck him.

One more slam of Hatter's hips and the coil in my body snapped. Ecstasy flooded my senses as I came with a deep groan, simultaneously squeezing Hatter's dick with convulsions, chocking Callister's cock with my hand, and gagging on Ransom's girth.

Hatter pulled out of my ass and slammed deep in my pussy, his restored magic crackling over my skin like lightning. Digging his fingers into my hips, he thrust hard and fast, letting out a low, drawn-out moan. His cock pulsed and twitched as he filled me with what felt like a month's worth of cum.

Ransom stood up, dragged his cock out of my mouth, and started fisting it furiously as he stepped behind me. Hatter slammed into me a few more times before abandoning my pussy. Ransom immediately took his place, sliding deep into me, stretching me wider.

"Fuck, it's wet in there," he groaned from behind. He pushed my hips to maneuver the front of my body closer to Callister.

"Tick tock, Alice," he growled as he gathered a handful of my hair with a tattooed fist. "Time's a-wasting."

Ignoring his triumphant smirk, I gripped his ridged length in both hands, then leaned down to swirl my tongue around the dark, tapered tip, tasting the tang of his pre-cum.

His insect cock was revolting, yet fascinating, the dark teal shimmering so much that I longed to simply study it. I used my tongue to explore the deep ridges that ran horizontally up the shaft, shuddering at the thought of this thing being in my pussy.

His hands fisted in my hair, forcing me to take him deeper. The ridges slid over my tongue, thick and unyielding, and I gagged.

Callister groaned, his fists tightening in her hair.

"That's it," he rasped. "Take it deeper, you little slut."

I hollowed my cheeks and sucked hard, ignoring my revulsion. Callister's cock swelled to an enormous size, pulsing hot and hard, but I didn't stop. I wasn't going to stop until he was helpless and vulnerable and coming all over me.

I would fucking *own* his orgasm.

I'd fuck him so good that he wouldn't even think about fucking anyone else.

Callister rammed his cock deeper down my throat, the ridges catching at the tender flesh in the corners of my mouth. Tears stung at my eyes, but I ignored them.

"I wish you could see yourself right now," he hissed above me. "Dripping full of cum, stuffed at both ends like a whore in heat."

My face burned but I ignored him. His words meant nothing. Only Ransom's pleasure-filled moans mattered.

His thrusts grew erratic, and I braced myself. "Close," he groaned. "So close, little bunny."

I arched my back to take him deeper, then redoubled my efforts on Callister's cock, sucking him further into my mouth. Callister grunted as his monstrous cock swelled even more.

With a shout, Ransom slammed into me and came, his release triggering Callister's own. Thick, hot spurts of semen flooded my mouth and pussy as Ransom and Callister simultaneously fell over the edge of euphoria.

I choked and sputtered on the thick, purple liquid coating my mouth, struggling and failing to swallow it all down. By the time their cocks had finished pulsing inside me, a strange warmth filled my body.

The wounds on Callister's body began fusing together right before my watery eyes. His clothes and bandages fell away, scarred flesh and broken tattoos made whole once more.

I sagged in relief, my duty fulfilled, as Ransom and Callister withdrew from my trembling body.

"Set up some mirrors for me," Callister told Ransom and Hatter. "I want this whore to watch me annihilate what's left of her filthy cunt."

"What? No!" I gasped.

"He's right," said Hatter, suddenly calm and collected. "We left it a proper mess."

"I meant Callister's healed! He doesn't need to come again!"

"Oh, yes I do," he growled. His smirk turned wicked, and he let out a sinister laugh. "Admit it. You want to know what it feels like to fuck the caterpillar."

"I only did what I did to save you," I said through gritted

teeth. My weak protests didn't stop Ransom and Hatter from setting up a few mirrors strategically placed around me.

"No, you're a greedy little slut, and you want to fuck the caterpillar," he murmured. "I'll prove it to you."

In a sudden burst of movement, Callister leaned down and grabbed me by the waist, lifting me off the floor with ease and settling me onto his lap.

His cock was already swollen, the ridged length stretching me deliciously as he effortlessly slid inside. The narrow base kept him from slipping back out.

"Tell me to stop," he taunted.

A broken moan fell from my lips at the fat, hot, wet, squishy sensation.

"That's what I thought . . . "

I gasped as the semi-soft spines covering his base ground against my sensitive clit, stimulating parts of me no human lover ever could. They sent sparks of pleasure and pain shooting through me.

"Look at you," Callister rasped, one hand sliding up to squeeze my tit. "So eager for my cock, even after taking two loads already." His hips rolled, grinding the spines against my clit in a way that made me see stars. "You're such a greedy little slut, aren't you?"

"No . . . "

"Yes, you are. Look at yourself," he urged. At that moment, Ransom brought one last mirror to the side of the sofa. Using some twisted magic, it showed me the view from a mirror just below my ass, reflecting the image of a wet, shiny, teal insect cock slipping in and out of my pussy.

I watched in fascination as pearly streams of cum from Hatter and Ransom dripped out of me. Slick, wet seed trickled down my slit and onto Callister's balls, then pooled onto the black velvet cushion of Ransom's sofa. I whimpered as the carnal, wet, primitive sounds of our fucking filled the air.

"Yes . . . such a fucking whore . . . " he moaned. "You love being full of our cum, don't you?"

I nodded, too ashamed to admit that he was right. He shifted the angle of his hips, grinding the spines harder against my clit until I moaned.

"You love fucking the caterpillar, don't you?"

I nodded again, and felt him swell inside me even bigger. The depraved thrill those words sent through me left me flushed with equal parts embarrassment and arousal. He wasn't wrong; even sated as I was, I craved more, craved the perverse ecstasy that only he could provide.

My hands found his tattooed shoulders, nails digging into the flawless ink. I rose up on shaking thighs before slamming back down onto his cock. We moaned in unison at the sensation, the ridges catching on my rim before popping free, only to repeat the motion as I rose again.

"Callister . . . " groaned Hatter. I turned my head to see both him and Ransom furiously fisting their hard cocks.

Callister's hands clamped onto my hips, stopping my movements. I whined in protest, trying to move, but his grip was unbreakable.

"Show me what a whore you truly are," he whispered into my ear, sending shivers of warmth down my neck. Another set of hands lifted me off his cock and impaled me onto another one. Ransom pumped once, twice, then let out a roar and flooded me with his molten demon heat. I arched my back to receive his offering.

"Fuck yeah—give it to me, my king!"

He thrust a few more times before pulling out. Then a third set of hands took control of my body as the Mad Hatter plunged inside, his indigo hair clinging to his sweaty cheekbones. He jackhammered hard and fast, erupting within seconds.

"Fucking *incredible* . . . " he gasped from below the brim of his tattered top hat. His single bright blue eye was gleaming with wonder. "Alice, you took that so well!"

In that moment, I was everything they ever wanted— completely uninhibited, and ready to be filled.

And I watched all of it happen, from every angle, in the reflection of the mirrors around me.

"My turn," Callister groaned as he guided the head of his cock to my gaping pussy. Creamy white seed coated his teal shaft as he slammed me back down on his lap, thrusting his freakish appendage into my core. Sloppy wet sounds became music to my ears as his insect dick sloshed and squished and plunged into the wetness. The entire area between his cock and his navel was splattered in splashes of jizz that wasn't his.

"You get off by knowing that I'm full of your friends' cum, don't you?" I asked. Callister's gaze zeroed in on me, but all he did was give me a faint snarl and thrust harder.

"Is that what turns you on?" I teased as I continued to bounce up and down on him. "Knowing that my pussy is filled to the brim with other guys' cum? You like feeling it slide all over your dick when you fuck me? You wanna fill me even more?"

A guttural, animalistic growl erupted from his tattooed chest as he thrust deep and held me in place. His cock began to swell even bigger inside me, startling me with the amount of pressure.

"What is that?"

"It's my knot," he growled, his voice low and possessed. "Stay put or you'll tear."

"It's gonna *tear* me?" I gasped, immediately trying to lift off of him, but his arms and his cock had me anchored in place.

"I said stay still!" he warned. "Trust me—you'll love it."

His eyes rolled into the back of his head and I started to panic.

Just then, the ridges of his cock began to flutter and move with a life all their own. They undulated along my G spot, caressing and massaging while the spikes palpated my clit, building the pressure inside me.

His grotesque cock pulsed and throbbed against my walls, thumping faster and harder, like a second heart. The ridges swelled even more, rubbing harder, as the knot stretched me to the point of pain. It was so tight. So hot.

I was so close.

I pressed my hips against him as hard as I could, grinding against the spikes. Tension simmered through my arms and legs, into my fingers and toes. I slid my hands under Callister's ass, desperately trying to draw him deeper into my body.

"That's it, Alice," he growled, eyes watching me with sadistic delight. "Show me what a slut you are and come for me."

The spikes and ridges ignited a familiar heat that coiled in my belly, building and building. I struggled to stay in that moment, but it was no use. More flickers of ridges lured me to the brink of ecstasy, then pushed me ruthlessly over the edge, setting my nerves on fire.

I broke my silence with a scream that might have been agony or ecstasy or both. My vision whited out as rapture consumed me. My inner walls convulsed around Callister's cock, squeezing tight. Through the haze of pleasure, I heard him surrender a guttural moan beneath the wet sound of flesh on flesh. I opened my eyes and saw a ferocious grin on Hatter's and Ransom's faces as they devoured the scene playing out in front of them.

Callister's eyes met mine, a wicked smirk curving his lips. He came with a roar, hot seed spurting deep within me. The swell of his knot locked us together, trapping his cum inside my body. Then he leaned forward and started to fuck, the force of him stealing my breath. The spines rubbed over my sensitive clit, each one drawing out more bursts of pleasure that had me crying with each thrust.

The pressure of his knot subsided as he drained his balls into me. He fucked me through our orgasms, his pace unrelenting.

"Again!" he demanded, slamming into my oversensitive flesh.

"I can't—it's too much!"

But even as I squirmed, trying to get away, my traitorous body responded. The tension built again, faster and sharper than before.

"Come again. *Now.*" His snarl was punctuated by a brutal thrust, sending me tumbling into another shattering orgasm.

Amidst the swirling vortex of colors and brilliant light, I was faintly aware of his groaning. With every muscle spasm and orgasmic contraction, I felt the hot splash of his release spill out of my pussy and onto his skin.

His head fell onto the back of the black velvet couch and I collapsed against him. His eyes were closed and his chest was heaving. My clit throbbed in the last few echoes of pleasure as more sticky fluid dripped out of me. I glanced down to see streaks of pearly white mingling within a dominant shade of thick purple.

Splaying my fingers over the hard muscle of his perfectly healed chest, I pushed myself up and stared at him in sheer wonder. I could hardly believe what I'd done.

I'd just fucked the caterpillar.

A soft groan caught my attention. Hatter was now dressed and sitting patiently in the nearby chair.

"Well that was certainly invigorating." He stretched his arms over his head, joints popping. "I feel like a new man."

Callister snorted. "As if anything could make you normal." But there was an edge of fondness to his words.

"You did wonderfully, Alice. Absolutely superb," said Ransom. He was also dressed and adjusting a gold club pin on his jacket lapel. "You've managed to bring them both back to perfect working order."

Warmth bloomed in my chest at his praise, and at the tender pride in his face as he looked at me. I felt so content in that moment.

So safe. So cherished.

He quirked a brow at the mess of fluids between us, but there was understanding in his eyes. An acknowledgment of the bonds that had been forged here today—bonds that would only grow stronger with time.

"You can get up now," Callister murmured beneath me, threatening to break the spell until he added, "unless you want to sit and stay awhile."

"I can barely feel my legs," I admitted as I tried—and failed— to crawl out of his lap.

He gave a nonchalant shrug and a smirk that was almost playful.

"I don't mind, as long as you make me another one of those pumpkin spice cigarettes."

I had one in my hand within seconds of imagining it, along with a glass of water that I immediately chugged.

A pair of brilliant green eyes appeared in front of me, floating in the air without a body.

"It seems I've missed quite the party . . . "

Oh fuck.

Chess.

My heart leapt at the sound of his voice, even as guilt flooded me. In the aftermath of such intense passion, I'd completely forgotten about him.

I felt terrible.

From the sticky warmth of Callister's lap, I watched him materialize before me. One hand was wrapped around the hilt of the Vorpal Sword. The other held a small black book. His curious eyes washed over the room, taking in the scene, his expression unreadable.

Only his mouth twitched.

"Honestly . . . I go to Hell for fifteen minutes, and *this* is what I come back to? Tsk, tsk, tsk."

"It was done purely in the name of restoring our health and sanity," Hatter chimed in with a cheeky grin.

"Sure it was," teased Chess, shaking his head. But fondness lurked in his eyes as he gazed at his friends.

And at me.

With his perpetual feline grace, he curled up in one corner of the sofa across from me and Callister, his gaze sharp as it swept over the tangle of limbs in front of him.

"Why, Callister . . . " he purred as he sniffed at the white cloud of pumpkin spiced smoke. "You look as though you've shed your old skin." Suddenly he frowned. "What's that on your face?"

Callister reached up with his free hand, inspecting his cheeks and forehead until a laugh rolled out of Chess's grin.

"Never mind. It's just a smile. No wonder it looked so strange on you."

Callister shot him a nasty look, but it quickly melted away into a satisfied smirk.

"I see you found the sword without any trouble," said Ransom. He stepped closer and held out his hand, but Chess ignored him.

"What is that in your hand?" Callister asked as he brought the cigarette to his perfect lips. "Is it a book?"

The grin on Chess's face disappeared, replaced by a clenched jaw.

"Of sorts. It's a diary. But oh, how I wish it was fiction."

Ransom's head snapped in his direction. He swiped out to snatch the little black book from Chess, but the Cheshire Cat had anticipated the move and abruptly disappeared.

"I have no time for your games, Chess," he warned with a growl.

"Ah, but you have time to fuck Alice the moment I leave the room?" came Chess's reply to my left. Then his voice drifted to my right. "You could've fucked her in front of me for all I care, but clearly you enjoy keeping secrets from me . . . from all of us, really."

Hatter frowned in confusion.

"What is he talking about?"

"Fuck if I know," Callister shrugged.

I finally climbed off his lap, astounded by what I saw in the mirror. My inner thighs were completely painted in transparent streaks of white and purple cum. I stared at my reflection and imagined that my body was as clean as the moment right after Ransom had hugged me.

Then I was.

Next, I imagined myself wearing black yoga pants, white sneakers, and a basic white t-shirt. If I needed to run from the Red Queen's army, I wasn't letting a stupid dress get in the way.

"I told you to get the Vorpal Sword, not dig through my private possessions!" Ransom snarled at the air above his head.

"I didn't snoop through your things," Chess replied, still invisible. "I was looking for the sword like you asked me to. The diary tumbled off the shelf right in front of me. Only the Fates could've made it fall open to a *very* particular page. How long have you been working with the Red Queen?"

A tense silence fell over the room as we all turned to Ransom. His usual calm demeanor was fraying at the edges.

"Ransom . . . what's he talking about?"

"It's none of your fucking business!" he snapped at me. His eyes were so cruel, so cold, that I was completely taken aback.

Callister flicked his cigarette aside, then slowly rose to his feet, positioning himself between me and the King of Clubs. I watched as a fresh set of new clothes wrapped around his hard, lean, rejuvenated body, covering most of his tattoos.

He lifted a powerful arm and raked his bright teal hair back into its signature pompadour, then rested his hands on his narrow hips. He squared his shoulders, jutting out his chin.

"I'm making it my fucking business."

Ransom stalked over, his dark gaze never leaving Callister's, yet the caterpillar didn't flinch a muscle. Hatter sidled up next to him, creating a veritable wall in front of me.

"If you're working with the Red Queen, we deserve to know. That includes Alice."

Ransom studied each of us in turn, his expression unreadable.

"Make good choices, Ransom," Chess purred condescendingly. "We don't have much time until the Red Queen arrives. I'm not returning the Vorpal Sword to someone who's collaborating with the worst enemy Wonderland has ever known."

The tension in the room was as thick as the smog in LA. Ransom clenched his fists as some of the stiffness left his body.

"It's not what you think. I'm not working with the Red Queen. I'm on your side. That's all you need to know."

"No . . . " Chess materialized in front of me, in front of his friends, the Vorpal Sword drawn at the ready. "If we're going to work together, we need to trust one another. And right now I don't trust you. Not entirely. Not after what I just read in your diary."

With a barely perceptible shake of his head, Ransom's scowl began to soften.

"I am *not* working with the Red Queen," he insisted. "You don't know the whole story."

Chess lifted a stern eyebrow.

"Then you'd better start talking. Otherwise, I will."

CHAPTER
THIRTEEN
ALICE

Ransom had just made a confession that left all of us speechless.

"You were *fucking* her?" Hatter repeated in disbelief. "You actually fucked the Red Queen? More than once?"

Ransom gave an exasperated shrug.

"I'm an incubus. It's what we do!"

"But she's psychotic!" Hatter argued. "And that's saying something, coming from me!"

"The crazy ones do tend to be wilder in bed," Callister said dryly.

Ransom rolled his eyes.

"I didn't fuck her after she went insane. It was a long, long time ago, back when she was relatively normal."

"But . . . *why?*"

Ransom pointed to his chest. "Incubus. Hot pussy. Do the math."

"That's not how I learned math," I replied, making Hatter snort a laugh. I pushed between him and Callister, realizing that Ransom wasn't the threat we'd feared. "Is an incubus not able to turn down sex?"

"Pretty much," Callister muttered under his breath.

"We feed on the different facets of sexual energy . . . on arousal and desire," Ransom explained. "Humans need food to fuel their bodies. Demons need energy. A lot of it. And incubi need a very specific type of energy. Hence the club of all clubs."

I tilted my head to one side as things began to click into place regarding the King of Clubs. The edging. The BDSM. The sex toys. The mirrors. The masked bunnies. The erotic performances set in the midst of a vibrant casino. Sex and money went hand in hand. I realized that Ransom had created The Rabbit Hole as a perfect sanctuary to thrive in.

"Tick tock, my friend. Tell them about the ring," Chess urged.

Ransom let out an irritated sigh.

"Fine. As I just said, Roxanne and I were lovers a long time ago. Dinah has always worked as her spy, keeping track of different Alices throughout the ages. I never paid much attention to that until I learned that this Alice was different from all the others." He paused as he glanced at me before continuing. "I started fucking Dinah for more information, but then Roxanne found out, and, as you can imagine, became insanely jealous. With me so far?"

"Yeah, but how am I different from the other Alices?" I asked. "Is it because I'm not a kid anymore?"

"No, but the reason isn't important right now," he said with an impatient wave of his hand. "Roxanne was furious when she learned that I was fucking Dinah, so she lured me into a night of passion. She must've drugged my wine, because I fell into such a deep sleep afterwards that when I woke up, my ring was gone."

"But you're wearing your ring," Callister pointed out.
Ransom lifted up his hand, showing off his gold pinky ring.

"It's a replica. I wear it so that nobody suspects the original Ring of Temptation is now worn by the Red Queen."

"She has your *ring?*" Callister hissed. "No wonder she's more powerful than ever!"

"I don't understand," I cut in. "What's the big deal about this ring?"

Hatter turned to me, conjuring himself a cup of tea.

"The Ring of Temptation is an ancient relic imbued with the power of seduction. It's the same power that all incubus demons have, only in concentrated form. Whoever wears it has a magic field of attraction around them. It's a bit like a love spell."

"It makes you bend over backwards to please them," added Callister. "You're more pliant. More willing to do their bidding. You're less likely to resist them or stand up for yourself."

"And given that an incubus feeds on sexual energy, this ring is rather useful for Ransom to have," said Chess. "But it would be too much power for any other creature. Especially a human. And giving that power to an unstable human like the Red Queen would be disastrous."

"Now you know why I never told anyone that she stole it from me. My plan was to kill her and take back my ring and nobody would be the wiser," Ransom quietly admitted. "I'm partly responsible for why things have become so dire in Wonderland this time around." He rested a sympathetic hand on Callister's shoulder. "She never killed the Red King until now. I'm so sorry about your brother."

Callister shoved his hand away like it was poison.

"Eat glass," he snarled through his teeth. Ransom took a step back, but looked him squarely in the eyes.

"If it would bring him back, I'd do it in a heartbeat."

Hatter took a long sip of his tea, then nearly spit it out.

"What's wrong?" I asked. "Was it too hot?"

"No, I just had an idea. Ransom, why not just fuck Roxanne again, drug her wine, and steal back your ring?"

Ransom shook his head.

"Believe me . . . I've tried getting it back on multiple occasions. But she's so paranoid that she won't let me anywhere near her."

"I guess it's a good thing she's on her way," Hatter quipped. "We should probably set up the masquerade ball while we still have time."

I couldn't help but feel a thrill of excitement mixed with my fear as I watched Ransom, Chess, Hatter, and Callister use their combined magic to transform the casino in a matter of minutes. The walls seemed to melt and shift before my eyes, taking on an opulent, otherworldly appearance. The chandeliers hanging from the ceiling bloomed into giant, multi-colored, crystalline flowers, casting a dim, seductive glow over the entire club.

The staff and guests of The Rabbit Hole were transformed as well, their clothing turning into elaborate, erotic costumes. Masks appeared on their faces, adding an element of mystery to the sensual atmosphere. I'd lost count of how long I'd been at The Rabbit Hole, but it was long enough that I felt totally comfortable wearing my bunny mask and a black push-up bustier. I added a pair of black lace cheeky panties with gold satin bows on the hips, and a pair of platform stilettos with gold bottoms.

From behind his mask, Hatter's blue eye blazed brighter than I thought possible as he looked me up and down.

"It's a good thing you weren't wearing that upstairs, or we never would've come down."

"Don't worry, I'll wear it again. Just for you."

Even if only for a moment, I let myself be swept up in the magical wonder of it all, temporarily forgetting the danger that loomed just outside the casino's doors.

"Remember, everyone," Ransom said, his voice heavy with

concern. "Stay alert, and stick to the plan. Chess, we're counting on you to be our invisible eyes and ears."

"I won't let you down," he said from somewhere above my head. I glanced up, but there was nothing there.

"Got it," I murmured, clutching the edges of my mask and trying not to let my nerves get the better of me. I wished I could be invisible like Chess.

But then I'd be a demon, and I wouldn't have a soul.

Did I even *need* a soul?

Maybe I wouldn't have one after I killed the Red Queen. I still couldn't believe I'd agreed to do it, but I was the only one with that power.

It seemed easier than killing the Jabberwocky. After seeing the vision of it that Ransom had shared with me, I never wanted to face it if I didn't have to.

My wicked boys were right—this was the better plan. Kill the Red Queen and be done with her forever.

As I looked around the transformed casino, I couldn't help but feel a sense of pride in our plan. The masquerade ball was a masterpiece of deception and seduction, a living, breathing distraction that would hopefully buy us enough time to confront the Red Queen on our own terms.

"Here's hoping this works," Hatter whispered to me as he made his top hat disappear and adjusted his own mask. His mismatched eyes revealed a combination of excitement and apprehension.

"Same," I replied, my voice barely a whisper. But despite the fear that gripped me, I knew one thing for certain—I'd do whatever it took to protect my wicked boys of Wonderland from the Red Queen.

The air crackled again and the doors of The Rabbit Hole flew open with a bang. There she stood . . . the infamous Red Queen, flanked by her soldiers, clad head to toe in red and black armor.

Hatter stiffened on my left, while Callister growled on my left.

Roxanne's helmet obscured her features, but I could feel the force of her glare through the eye slits. She raised the front to reveal a cruel scowl at the sight of the lavish masquerade ball.

It was the last thing she was expecting to see.

"WHERE IS ALICE?" her voice boomed above the music and laughter, until everything went silent.

Ransom glided forward, a vision of predatory grace in his elegant black and gold mask. "Long time no see, Your Majesty. Whoever are you referring to? You don't mean *the* Alice, do you?"

"Do not play games with me, demon!" the Red Queen hissed. "I know Alice is here! Surrender her at once, or I will tear this place apart brick by fucking brick until I find her!"

My heart raced as I watched the exchange, my entire being focused on keeping my presence hidden. I was grateful for the bunny mask that covered my face, allowing me to blend into the crowd of costumed guests.

"I'm sorry, Your Majesty, but if Alice was at my club, I'd be the first to know. Whoever gave you this information was sadly misinformed," he said with a diplomatic smile. "But since you've come all this way, you and your soldiers are more than welcome to join in on the festivities. I'm sure you and your men are tired."

"Are you calling me old?" she asked through bared teeth.

"Hardly," Ransom crooned. "You're a vision of desire. As a matter of fact, I was just reminiscing about you earlier today. You've been working so very hard. You deserve to relax. There's plenty of wine and refreshments to go around."

He waved over a server carrying a tray of champagne and handed Roxanne a glass.

She refused to take it.

"Do you seriously expect me to believe you?" she sneered, her eyes narrowing suspiciously.

"Believe what you like," Ransom replied, undeterred as he

took a hearty drink from the glass. "But as I said, Alice isn't here. I do hope you and your soldiers will stay and enjoy the masquerade ball. After all, the more, the merrier."

"He's right about that," Callister murmured as he gave my ass a hard squeeze. It was all I could do to smother my laugh.

Raising his glass of champagne, Ransom signaled for the ball to resume. Within seconds, the music and the chatter and the games picked up right where they'd left off.

With Hatter and Callister by my side, I watched as Roxanne looked around the room. Her gaze lingering on a trio of scantily clad bunnies who were setting up for a live sex performance on the nearby stage.

"Very well," she said with a painted-on smile. "We shall stay . . . for now. Dinah, where are you? I need a wardrobe change!"

My blood ran cold at the sight of my long-time personal assistant rushing over to help the Red Queen. Dinah used to make me her signature magic blue smoothies every morning. Now she was a stylist to the biggest bitch in Wonderland.

I watched in disbelief as she snapped her fingers and transformed Roxanne's armor into a stunning crimson gown. Her helmet was replaced by a sinister, bejeweled mask that perfectly matched her menacing aura. Strings of red rubies wrapped around her throat, tumbling over her collarbones like shiny drops of blood.

"Holy shit—how did she do that?" I whispered to Hatter. "Isn't Dinah human like me?"

"No. She's fae like me," he replied. "No relation."

"Why is she here? What if it's to identify me?"

"You're mostly likely right, but that's why the middle of a masquerade ball is the perfect place to be," he assured me. "You're not alone."

I swallowed hard, my mouth gone dry. But Hatter was right. I'd seen my reflection and had barely recognized myself.

I could do this.

And I wasn't alone.

I watched Roxanne lift a finger of warning to Ransom, then use her fingertip to trace an 'X' over his heart before dragging it down his chest.

"But know this, Ransom—if I find out that you have lied to me, there will be hell to pay."

"Duly noted," he replied, sounding almost bored. "Please let me know if there's anything you'd like from me. Anything that I actually have in my possession, that is," he added with a seductive wink. "Otherwise, enjoy the masquerade."

With that, he stepped away, disappearing into the crowd. I followed him as long as I could, but Roxanne was such a commanding force that it was impossible for me to look away from her for very long.

"Soldiers," she said, her voice dripping with malice. "Keep your eyes peeled for Alice and her known accomplices, Chess, Hatter, and Callister. They may very well be here tonight, or soon will be. This is quite the spectacle."

My heart hammered in my chest as I watched the soldiers fan out across the casino floor. Their eyes scanned the crowd with ruthless intensity, leaving me feeling vulnerable and exposed . . .

Leaving me feeling like it was just a matter of time before they found me.

"Was I convincing enough?"

I gasped and whipped around to see Ransom standing behind me. I almost smacked him, but I stopped myself in time. The last thing I wanted to do was draw attention to myself.

"You were fantastic," said Hatter.

Even Callister gave a reluctant nod from underneath the hooded cloak he wore. Being covered in so many distinctive tattoos, it was the easiest option. The deep hood covered his teal hair perfectly.

"She seems more interested in getting fucked than turning your club inside out."

"It's true," said Chess from above us. He was still invisible, floating around like a cloud. "She's already giving requests to the sex performers."

"Lovely, simply lovely," Ransom hummed as he waved a hand over his glass and replaced the champagne with water. "So far, everything is going to plan. Did you see how she ran her fingers down my chest?"

"That doesn't mean she wants to fuck you." I resisted the urge to glare at him. "It looked like she wanted to rip your heart out."

"Give her some wine and some time, and she'll definitely want this," he said with a smug smirk. "Then I'll bring her upstairs where you'll all be waiting to carry out the rest of the plan. It's brilliant."

"It's risky. I wasn't expecting so many soldiers."

Ransom glanced down at me, letting some of his dark hair fall into his eyes. Fuck, he was gorgeous. I don't know why he even needed that magic ancient Ring of Temptation.

"Have you ever been a soldier?"

I shook my head.

"They're away from home for months and months at a time. They get bored. They get lonely. They get tired of draining their balls into their own hands."

Callister and Hatter snickered and nodded in agreement.

"Now they're at The Rabbit Hole, where every desire they can imagine is just waiting to be enjoyed. Waiting to be had . . . again, and again . . . and again. How hard do you *really* think they're going to look for any of you? Why, there goes one of them right now. They'll be dropping like flies in no time at all."

I followed his gaze to see a soldier in a mask leading a giggling bunny into a dark corner of the room. Another one was buying a drink for a masked man standing at a roulette wheel, his finger-tips dancing along his back.

Ransom's lips curled into a sly smile. "Roxanne's soldiers will never find you amidst all the costumes and chaos and pleasure."

"She doesn't need to find me," I pointed out, remembering a movie I'd recently seen. "All she needs to do is start killing people until I give myself up."

Ransom waved a dismissive hand. "She won't do that. Not yet, at least. Roxanne loves games, and she'll want to draw this out as long as possible." His gaze darkened. "But we must be ready to spring into action the moment she makes her move."

His words didn't do much to soothe my anxiety. The waiting and watching were almost worse than knowing what I was supposed to do with the Vorpal Sword.

Ransom leaned down and nuzzled against my cheek. "Patience, bunny. The time will come soon enough. I'm going to go mingle with my guests. I suggest you do the same. Don't worry—Callister and Hatter won't leave you alone for a second. Chess will let you know when it's time to act."

Taking a deep breath, I grabbed Callister's hand and forced my feet to move, leading him onto the crowded dance floor. I let myself be swept up in the beat of the music, and I melted against his hard, muscular heat, our bodies moving in time with the seductive rhythm.

"Ransom sure trained you well," he said in my ear as one song blended into another. I looked up into his eyes and saw pure lust staring back at me.

"How do you mean?"

"I didn't think you'd have the stamina to take three cocks in one sitting, but you proved me wrong. We didn't exactly go easy on you."

"Yeah, I can tell. I'm pretty sore right now."

Callister's eyes puckered as if he was caught between pleasure and pain. Then he pulled me close, dancing slow, grinding his hard-on against me through our clothes.

"You shouldn't tell me things like that. It just makes me want to fuck your bruised cunt even harder."

Although I ached from what he and his friends had done to me earlier, heat began to pool in my core. I wrapped my bare arms around him, moving in harmony with him on the dance floor. I pressed my face against the side of his hood.

"I love knowing how bad you wanna fuck my poor, aching pussy. You guys fucking *wrecked* me down there. No wonder you wanted to fuck me last."

"Wait until Chess gets in on the fun. Your pussy will be nothing but a stretched out, cum-filled, gaping, dripping gash between your legs."

"Is that what you want?" I teased. Callister groaned and I had my answer. "You want me broken in and loaded with hot, wet cum just for you?"

He groaned again, this time louder.

"Fuuuuuuck . . ."

He flipped me around so that my back was pressed against him. I half expected him to cut a hole in his cloak and slip his cock into me.

Instead, he maneuvered his fingers through the leg of my panties and slipped a finger inside my wetness.

"How are you so fucking tight after what we did to you?"

"I dunno. I do kegels. Maybe that's it?" Just to prove my point, I squeezed him as hard as I could. I imagined trapping his finger inside my magic pussy and not letting go.

"I hate to break up all the fun, but it's time," said Chess from above me. I looked up and saw nothing.

"Can you let me go?" Callister asked. "My finger's stuck."

"You're kidding, right?"

"Wish I was." I tried stepping away from him, but he was right. My pussy was clamped down on him like a vise.

I closed my eyes and imagined my pussy relaxing and opening up, ready to take any cock that it encountered. Within a few seconds, Callister's finger slid out, leaving a warm wet trail on my inner thigh. He brought it to his mouth and sucked it clean.

Suddenly his head jerked to one side, like someone had slapped him.

"Enough screwing around!" Chess hissed. "Ransom's about to bring the Red Queen upstairs. Hatter's waiting in the hall. Now hurry!"

My heart pounded so hard in my chest that I half expected it to burst through my ribs and flop all around the tile floor of Ransom's bedroom. I positioned myself in as seductive of a pose as I could think of, draping my legs across his black silk bedding, taking care not to poke holes in it with my spiky stilettos.

Hatter and Callister peered out from behind their hiding spots in the room.

"Ready?" Hatter asked, his voice remarkably steady despite the situation. I nodded, swallowing hard, trying to fight off the fear that threatened to consume me.

"Yeah. Let's do this," I whispered. Using my imagination, I replaced my apprehension with cold determination.

I could do this.

And I would win.

I heard Roxanne's voice echoing down the hall as she and Ransom approached the room.

"Do you want my men to watch us, or stand guard outside?"

"I want what you want," Ransom said with a clear undertone of hunger.

"Oh, I suppose it's better to have them wait outside the door.

But I insist you leave it open. I'd like them to hear that new bunny of yours squeal."

My stomach flipped at Roxanne's words, and not in a good way. I didn't trust her. I lifted the pillow one last time to make sure the Vorpal Sword was right where Chess and I had put it.

It was.

I licked my lips just as Ransom and Roxanne stepped into the room.

"Here she is," he declared, looking at me like I was a piece of custom-built furniture instead of a person. "My newest bunny. What do you think of her?"

"Hard to say. Let's see how she measures up against me."

Roxanne flung her gown off like a robe, letting it fall to the floor beneath her gorgeous body. She pulled off her mask and narrowed her eyes at me. Her sharp, fine features were surrounded by a mane of intense red hair that had been swept up off her neck.

All that she wore was the ruby necklace and a gold ring on her index finger.

It was the exact same as Ransom's pinky ring—the replica he wasn't wearing.

"Come over here and let me look at you," Roxanne ordered. Ransom gave me a stern look but I ignored it.

I knew what to do.

"Yes, my queen."

I slipped off the bed and got down on all fours, keeping my head bowed.

"Stand up."

I stood.

Roxanne walked around me in a slow circle, scrutinizing every inch of my body. She slapped my ass a few times, making my cheeks bounce. Her cold fingers unfastened my bustier and pinched my tits until I wanted to punch her.

All I did was smile.

She didn't know who I really was, but I was still the bait to help lure her into our twisted web.

"Very firm," she said to Ransom. "I can see why you chose her. Nice legs as well. How's her cunt?"

"Exceptional," he replied. "Pink. Delicious. Tight."

"Is that so?" She turned to me with a cruel gleam in her eyes, and I immediately averted my gaze. "Take off your panties."

I hesitated for second, but then did as I was told.

"Show me this exceptional pussy of yours," Roxanne demanded. Head bowed, I spread my legs apart, wondering why the hell I'd agreed to do this. Why couldn't I have just hidden under the bed and waited for the right moment?

The Red Queen stepped closer, reaching out to slide her fingertips up and down my outer labia. Then she spread it apart, narrowing her eyes.

"Such a pretty little cunt, although it's not as pretty as mine."

"Nobody's cunt is as pretty as yours," Ransom agreed, and I couldn't help feeling a brutal sting of jealousy. Even though I knew he was lying, it hurt.

Unless he wasn't lying.

No, I couldn't think like that.

"Is her pussy as tight as mine?"

"Not even close, my queen."

Again, that sting of jealousy hit me harder than it should. He'd better not be lying. I was starting to get pissed off.

"Let's just see about that."

Before I knew it, Roxanne's finger thrust deep inside me, coating itself in all the slippery arousal that Callister had created down on the dance floor.

"My, my, she's certainly slick in there. I can see why you're so impressed with your new toy, Ransom."

I closed my eyes, hating her pumping her finger in me, wishing it was Ransom's or Callister's exploring me instead. Fucking bitch didn't even bother to take off her ring . . .

Suddenly I grinned, humming to myself.

Still pressing against my inner walls, Roxanne let out a contemptuous laugh. "I hate to say it, but I don't think her cunt is very tight at all—oooh!"

She didn't think I was tight?

I'd show her.

I clamped down on her finger as hard as I could, imagining a literal vise inside my pussy. Roxanne gasped in surprise, her eyes widening in shock as she tried—and failed—to pull her finger out.

"Ransom!" she hissed. "Control your toy!"

"Off the bed," he told me, pointing at the floor. "Now."

I pulled Roxanne's finger out of me, then rolled off the bed and stood near the headboard, obediently waiting for my services to be needed.

My stomach twisted into an anxious knot as Ransom gently pushed Roxanne down onto the edge of the bed. His hands ghosted over her bare skin, teasing her nipples as his mouth feverishly made its way down between her thighs. In the reflection of all the mirrors around us, I watched her long legs spread open as he bent forward to deliver his delicious heat, bathing her clit with his skillful tongue.

Anger burned through me at watching the incubus do what he did best. If it had been any other random, nameless woman, I wouldn't have cared. But it was Roxanne, the Red Queen who'd made everyone in Wonderland miserable. She'd killed Callister's brother. She'd tortured him. I saw firsthand what kind of sick, twisted evil she was capable of.

Roxanne let out a throaty groan as Ransom slipped two fingers inside her and continued to lick and suck. His gaze met mine, his eyes burning with intensity.

I couldn't read his thoughts, but I knew exactly what he was thinking.

Now.

I shuddered, then blinked as I took in the sight of the Red

Queen's neck, vulnerable and exposed on Ransom's bed. The strings of rubies fell down her throat like the trickles of blood that were destined to replace them. Her eyes squeezed shut in pleasure as she sank her fingers into his hair. Her forefinger still glistened with my clear, slippery wetness.

Fucking cunt, I thought to myself. *We'll see who has the last laugh. This is Ransom's house . . . and the house always wins.*

In between wet slurps and licks, Ransom moaned, catching my attention with his demonic gaze once more.

Do it! Now!

With a surge of adrenaline, my hand slipped under the pillow and wrapped around the hilt of the Vorpal Sword. It didn't make a sound as I pulled the blade out from between the silk pillowcases and sheets. I took it in both hands and raised my arms, channeling all my strength into the blow that would end the Red Queen's reign of terror once and for all.

I lunged forward and brought the sword down as hard as I could, slicing through the air with near perfect precision. The blade came down hard on Roxanne's neck . . .

But it was just the tip.

Her eyes flew open as a handful of red beads rolled off her neck and onto the black silk beneath her. A razor-thin line appeared on her neck, then started to bleed.

She sat upright and stared at me, my sword in hand, and for a moment we all froze. Rubies from her broken necklace went flying all over the floor, their sounds making sharp, distinct, crystalline notes in the air. They were so small, so delicate, and yet their innocent chimes filled the room until the last one fell.

"Finish her, Alice!" Ransom hissed as he grabbed the Red Queen's arms and shifted into his demon form.

Roxanne's face broke out in absolute fury as she realized who I was, and what I was holding.

Then she let out a bloodcurdling scream, and all hell broke loose.

CHAPTER
FOURTEEN

ALICE

"GUARDS! SEIZE THEM!"

Trembling and terrified of failure, I swung for the Red Queen's neck one more time as Chess, Hatter, and Callister blocked the two guards from intervening. At the last second, Roxanne dodged behind Ransom's thick, muscular arm and my blade only sank into her shoulder.

The room erupted into chaos as over a dozen soldiers pushed through the door, armed to the teeth. Steel met steel and magic clashed against magic, filling the air with sparks and metallic clangs.

With my entire body shaking, I swung the Vorpal Sword at Roxanne a third time, slicing a shallow cut down her back as she thrashed beneath Ransom. I just didn't have the strength, the aim, the focus.

Streams of color shot past me as spells and arrows were hurled in my direction. Ransom shoved Roxanne to the floor and grabbed me around the waist, shielding me from harm with his massive wings.

"I've got you," he growled as an arrow tore through one of his wings. "Nobody's going to hurt you. Not while I'm alive."

"Ransom, what do we do?" I yelled, desperately trying to maintain my grip on the sword as the world around us became a whirlwind of violence.

"Follow me! Stay close!" he shouted back, summoning a wall of shadows to shield us from oncoming attacks.

Roxanne lunged at me, her eyes insane with rage. I kicked her in the leg as hard as I could, sinking my stiletto heel into her flesh. Ransom turned and threw her to the floor like a rag doll, only for a soldier to take her place.

I caught a glimpse of Chess towering above the fray in his giant beast form, each swing of his massive paws shredding soldiers like they were made of paper. His body shimmered with every swipe, constantly vanishing and reappearing in a different spot, making it impossible for the guards to anticipate his moves.

Hatter cackled maniacally as he conjured a blinding torrent of electric blue lightning that sent a group of soldiers flying backward. Their swords and crossbows clattered to the floor and their bones audibly cracked on impact as they landed in broken, twisted heaps.

"Nice one, Hatter!" Callister shouted, slamming his fist into a soldier's face with such brutal force that both eyeballs shot out of their sockets. The caterpillar's tattoos came alive, insects stinging and snakes biting soldiers as if drawing power from the violence surrounding them.

The floor was carpeted with corpses, their blood mixing with brain matter and intestines until it was impossible to tell one from the other. Blood pooled on the slick tile floor into thick red puddles. One soldier slipped in the blood and impaled himself on his own sword. So many bodies littered the floor that they were starting to pile up and block the door.

Yet more soldiers came pushing through.

"Where the hell are they all coming from?" I gasped in disbelief, my mind racing as more and more soldiers poured into the room. There were just too many. We were outnumbered and surrounded, hopelessly trapped. All my senses went numb with overwhelm at the shrieks of battle and the smell of blood and sweat hanging heavy in the air.

"Doesn't matter," Ransom gritted out, taking another arrow that was aimed at me. "We need to get out of here!"

"Agreed," Chess growled, his voice strained as he continued to fend off the attackers. "This isn't going to end well if we stay."

"Callister!" Ransom snarled as we made our way to the black velvet sofas. "Take Alice through here! We'll be right behind you!"

He shoved me into Callister's arms, then outstretched his wings to shield us both as more arrows flew in our direction. I sucked in a breath as Callister held on tight and jumped into one of the mirrors they'd set up during our fuckfest from earlier.

I braced myself for the impact of shattered glass, but our reflection swallowed us into darkness. Then I was lying on a cold stone floor, watching the battle rage from the other side of the mirror. Callister's chest heaved against my back, panting hard as he refused to let me go. Our breath rose like smoke in the frosty air.

I watched, helpless, as Ransom roared in rage while arrows tore through his beautiful demon wings. Still, he kept them fully outstretched as Hatter ran through the mirror like it was a golden doorway to safety. Then suddenly he was with us, panting lungfuls of steam into the cold air that surrounded us.

Chess went absolutely feral, tearing into soldiers with his teeth, with his claws, shoving the pile of bodies against the doorway until it was sufficiently blocked.

"Run for it!" Ransom yelled at him. Chess shifted back into his human shape before leaping through the mirror. Ransom folded his wings and dove after him just as another handful of arrows went flying at us. The pile of corpses blocking the door was beginning to fall apart.

"What do we do?" I panicked.

"Just wait. Look." Callister lifted an arm and pointed to a spot left of the center of the mirror. An arrow was lodged in the glass, and a spiderweb of hairline fractures was snaking across the mirror, shooting out in every direction.

I heard the sound of breaking glass before I realized that the image of Ransom's bedroom was falling away, piece by piece. Shards of glass in every shape and size tumbled down and shattered on the black and gold tiles. The sight of the mutilated bodies and the velvet sofas and the pools of blood disappeared until all we were looking at was an empty gold frame.

Strong, cold fingers pried the Vorpal Sword from my shaking, clutching hands, but Callister didn't try to stop it.

A swirling motion of gleaming platinum and black moved faster than my eyes could register what it was. The gold frame in front of us shook, then collapsed in pieces as if it had been cut by a laser.

My eyes focused on the figure standing above the remains of the mirror. Black armor accented in the palest shade of silver was molded perfectly to a muscular male body. A long black cloak hung from a powerful set of broad shoulders, draped elegantly around his armor. He held the Vorpal Sword with so much skill and control that it gave me the impression he knew the blade better than I ever would.

Shiny, long cascades of platinum white hair fell down both sides of his flawlessly chiseled face, making the startling red color of his eyes impossible to ignore.

His cold gaze flicked down to me, holding me in a brief, hypnotic spell. I couldn't look away even if I'd wanted to. I wondered if this was how a fly felt after it had been paralyzed by a spider's bite . . . waiting for the venom to slowly liquify its body and turn it into food.

Whatever this terrifying creature was—he wasn't human. He wasn't fae. I wasn't even sure if he was a demon, but he scared me enough that I was grateful to not be alone.

Unfazed by the lightning-quick speed that he'd used to slash the mirror frame apart, Hatter walked up to him and gave him an appreciative slap on the back like they were old drinking buddies.

"Thanks, Jack. I owe you one."

"You owe much more than one," he murmured so quietly that I barely heard him. "It's fine. I stopped counting years ago."

"Sorry to break up the reunion, but I'm worried about Ransom," said Chess, who was kneeling down by his side. Ransom was conscious, but he was clearly in agony. His wings were full of gaping holes, oozing with black slime.

"Is that his blood?" I asked, reaching out to touch.

A cold hand wrapped around my wrist, pulling me away from him.

"Don't touch him," Jack warned.

How the actual *fuck* had he appeared by my side so fast?

His piercing red eyes seemed to see through my very soul. "He's been shot by a large number of poisoned arrows. They're rotting his flesh away. They'll do the same to you if you touch his wounds."

"But we have to do *something*. He saved us all!"

Jack gave an imperceptible nod.

"Yes. I saw that. We'll bring him straight to the Queen. She'll know exactly how to heal him."

"No!" I cried out. "Are you insane?" I tried yanking my arm out of Jack's grasp, but his hand was like stone.

"He means the White Queen, Alice," Callister explained as he, Chess, and Hatter used their magic to levitate Ransom and put him on a floating stretcher. "We're nowhere near the Red Queen. We're not even in the Kingdom of Hearts and Roses anymore."

"Then where the fuck are we?" I huffed angrily.

"You're in the Kingdom of Diamonds and Ice," Jack replied before letting me go. "Welcome to the White Queen's court."

The fear I'd felt just seconds ago began to fade away, replaced by curiosity.

"Are you by any chance the White Knight?"

His mouth shifted in a whisper of movement, the closest thing I might get to a smile. Blood red eyes sparkled at me with icy charm.

"What gave it away?" he deadpanned before tossing his long white hair out of his face.

His gaze drifted slowly down my body, then back up to me. Somewhere in those cold, red eyes, a predatory flicker burned. And somehow, I got the feeling that this kind of predator battled a hunger that would never be satisfied.

"You seem cold. Would you like something warmer to wear?"

"I'm fine."

Just then, a cool breeze blew over us, giving me chills while catching a few strands of his hair. It glittered in the soft blueish light, making him look almost angelic.

But there was nothing angelic in the way Jack was looking at me.

He looked at me like I was prey.

To be fair, I *was* completely naked, aside from one broken high heel and my half-mangled bunny mask.

"Try this on," he said, and held out the Vorpal Sword. Hanging off the end was a slinky, fuzzy scrap of white fabric. I picked it up and held it out for inspection, then wrinkled my nose. It seemed to be some kind of tank top dress.

"You're joking, right?"

"Try it on," he repeated. "Take off your shoe first."

Rolling my eyes, I kicked off the broken stiletto and pulled the fuzzy tank top over my head. I'd just barely tugged it into place when it started to grow and morph around the curves of my body.

Suddenly I was wearing a long dress that felt like the most exquisite cashmere against my skin. Fur-lined white boots lifted my bare feet off the cold floor, then crawled up to my mid-thighs. A luxurious white fur coat wrapped around me like a hug, and my mask dissolved into tiny ice crystals before evaporating into nothingness.

"Shall we go see the White Queen?" he asked as he turned to Chess, Callister, and Hatter. "She's in the East Wing. It's not far from here at all."

With Ransom floating along on his airborne stretcher, we made our way into a large, open, alabaster corridor. A star-studded night sky arched across the ceiling, flickering with the purples and blues and greens of an aurora borealis dancing over our heads. Everything seemed to shimmer with a coating of diamond dust, casting us in an ethereal glow.

It was cold, but it was beautiful.

I'd felt safe with my wicked boys, but this place felt like a sanctuary. I'd found the Vorpal Sword. I'd learned discipline and humility from Ransom, among other things. Now I'd met the White Knight.

I tried to stay optimistic that he wouldn't scare me so much once I got to know him better. After all, I hadn't been so sure about Callister, but he'd come around.

Eventually.

"Hey, thanks for the outfit, Jack," I said, pulling the coat closer around me as we walked along. "I'm Alice, by the way."

His red gaze slid down to me.

"Yes, I know who you are. You're incredibly late."

"Better late than never."

His lips parted, revealing a sardonic grin . . . and a long pair of sharp white fangs.

My stomach turned as I realized what he was . . .

And what I was.

Prey.

**Pssst . . .
I need your opinion. Got a sec?**

Leaving reviews is one of the most kickass ways to support authors. You're also helping other readers decide if our books are right for them. If you have a minute, I'd LOVE a review from you!

Review King of Clubs on Amazon

Review King of Clubs on Goodreads

Thanks so much!

Jekka

JEKKA'S WILDE ONES

Desperate for more?

Join Jekka's Wilde Ones!

Get immediate access to Jekka's private Facebook group, character art, the spiciest new Fantasy & PNR books, and be notified of new releases before anyone else.

Become a Wilde One at jekkawilde.com/newsletter

About the Author

Jekka Wilde (aka the Duchess of Depravity) reigns supreme in her frostbitten kingdom in the northern US, where she's practically *forced* to write steamy stories to stay warm.
A self-proclaimed caffeine aficionado, she can often be found snuggled under a blanket fortress, sipping a matcha latte that's almost as hot as the scorching scenes in her books.
In a house that's part library, part shoe warehouse, Jekka's motto in life and literature is 'Why Choose?'—a philosophy that's evident in every romance she writes. The only thing filthier than her humor is the plot.
If you're looking for sweet romance, keep walking. But if you're ready for a wild, witty, and wicked ride, congratulations! You've just found your new favorite author.

9 781964 291055